Emily Harvale lives in — although she would prefer to live in French Alps ... or Canada ... or anywhere that has several months of snow. Emily loves snow almost as much as she loves Christmas. Having worked in the City (London) for several years, Emily returned to her home town of Hastings where she spends her days writing ... and wondering if it will ever snow. You can contact her via her website, Facebook or Instagram.

There is also a Facebook group where fans can chat with Emily about her books, her writing day and life in general. Details can be found on Emily's website.

Author contacts:
www.emilyharvale.com
www.twitter.com/emilyharvale
www.facebook.com/emilyharvalewriter
www.instagram.com/emilyharvale

***

Scan the code above to see all Emily's books on Amazon

Also by this author

The Golf Widows' Club
Sailing Solo
Carole Singer's Christmas
Christmas Wishes
A Slippery Slope
The Perfect Christmas Plan
Be Mine
It Takes Two
Bells and Bows on Mistletoe Row

Lizzie Marshall series:
Highland Fling – book 1
Lizzie Marshall's Wedding – book 2

Goldebury Bay series:
Ninety Days of Summer – book 1
Ninety Steps to Summerhill – book 2
Ninety Days to Christmas – book 3

Hideaway Down series:
A Christmas Hideaway – book 1
Catch A Falling Star – book 2
Walking on Sunshine – book 3
Dancing in the Rain – book 4

Hall's Cross series
Deck the Halls – book 1
The Starlight Ball – book 2

Michaelmas Bay series
Christmas Secrets in Snowflake Cove – book 1
Blame it on the Moonlight – book 2

Lily Pond Lane series
The Cottage on Lily Pond Lane – four-part serial
Part One – New beginnings
Part Two – Summer secrets

Part Three – Autumn leaves
Part Four – Trick or treat
Christmas on Lily Pond Lane
Return to Lily Pond Lane
A Wedding on Lily Pond Lane
Secret Wishes and Summer Kisses on Lily Pond Lane

Wyntersleap series
Christmas at Wynter House – Book 1
New Beginnings at Wynter House – Book 2
A Wedding at Wynter House – Book 3
Love is in the Air – spin off

Merriment Bay series
Coming Home to Merriment Bay – Book 1
(four-part serial)
Part One – A Reunion
Part Two – Sparks Fly
Part Three – Christmas
Part Four – Starry Skies
Chasing Moonbeams in Merriment Bay – Book 2
Wedding Bells in Merriment Bay – Book 3

Seahorse Harbour series
Summer at my Sister's – book 1
Christmas at Aunt Elsie's – book 2
Just for Christmas – book 3
Tasty Treats at Seahorse Bites Café – book 4
Dreams and Schemes at The Seahorse Inn – book 5
Weddings and Reunions in Seahorse Harbour – book 6

Clementine Cove series
Christmas at Clementine Cove – book 1
Broken Hearts and Fresh Starts at Cove Café – book 2

Copyright © 2022 by Emily Harvale.

Emily Harvale has asserted her right to be identified as the author of this work.

All rights reserved. No part of this publication may be reproduced, stored in a retrieval system, or transmitted, in any form or by any means, without the prior written permission of the publisher.

All names, characters, organisations, businesses, places and events other than those clearly in the public domain, are fictitious and any resemblance to real persons, living or dead, events or locales, is purely coincidental.

ISBN 978-1-909917-85-9

Published by Crescent Gate Publishing

Print edition published worldwide 2022
E-edition published worldwide 2022

Cover design by JR and Emily Harvale

Emily Harvale

Friendships Blossom in Clementine Cove

CRESCENT GATE PUBLISHING

Acknowledgements

My grateful thanks go to the following:

Christina Harkness for her patience and care in editing this book.
My webmaster, David Cleworth who does so much more than website stuff.
My cover design team, JR.
Luke Brabants. Luke is a talented artist and can be found at: www.lukebrabants.com
My wonderful friends for their friendship and love. You know I love you all.
All the fabulous members of my Readers' Club. You help and support me in so many ways and I am truly grateful for your ongoing friendship. I wouldn't be where I am today without you.
My Twitter and Facebook friends, and fans of my Facebook author page. It's great to chat with you. You help to keep me (relatively) sane!

Map of Clementine Cove

There's an interactive map, with more details,
on my website: www.emilyharvale.com

For David Cleworth.
Because I can never say 'Thank You'
enough. So once again, 'Thank You!'

Chapter 1

Stella Pinkheart picked up her mail from the coir doormat where it had landed and shuffled through the pile of envelopes, stopping when she spotted a large postcard of the French Riviera. It was from Marian, Stella knew that, but her heart skipped half a beat, nonetheless, although she was fully aware of the fact that it could not possibly have been from ... *him*. It was ludicrous of her to think it might be, even for a nano-second. Especially after all these years.

Stella slowly inhaled a calming breath, hastily flipped the postcard over and tried to decipher Marian's scrawl. She smiled and shook her head, remembering how Marian's penmanship always suffered when the girl was excited. Not that Marian was a girl any longer. She was a grown woman in her thirties, however much Stella might still see her as the orphaned teenaged daughter of two of Stella's dearest, but long-departed, friends.

Stella cleared her throat and read the spidery writing. Marian was evidently genuinely happy and loving life aboard Parker Sanderson's yacht, *The Dream*. She had told Stella as much in the texts she had sent previously, but seeing Marian's words in her own handwriting made them more real somehow. Marian didn't even seem to mind having to be at the beck and call of the wealthy clients who paid Parker eye-watering sums to sail them around the Mediterranean and be waited on hand and foot by Captain Parker and his crew. That pleased Stella immensely and also brought a sigh of relief.

To say that Stella had been surprised back in February, when Marian had announced her intention to join the man she had fallen in love with, on his luxury yacht, and cruise around the Med until at least September, was an understatement. Marian had been her own boss and run her own business, Cove Café for more than fifteen years and Stella was concerned that the transition from boss to crew member might be a difficult adjustment. Not only that, Marian had lived in Clementine Cove her entire life and Stella was worried Marian would quickly feel homesick. Judging by the way Marian enthused about life onboard *The Dream*, it seemed Stella needn't have worried on either score.

Nevertheless, Stella had been astonished to discover that Marian had agreed to hand over the keys of her beloved Cove Café, to Archer Rhodes, and that Marian and Archer, together with Archer's chef, Bentley had a new business plan for Marian's café. They intended to expand Archer's hugely popular restaurant in his pub, The Bow and Quiver, by opening a Café Bistro in a refurbished Cove Café. Bentley would be running the place, alongside the pub restaurant, but it would only open in the evenings and weekends. During the day, it would still be run as a café, although at the time of Marian's departure it had not been decided who, exactly, would be doing that once the alterations and redecoration were completed. Cove Cottage – and Cove Café had meant the world to Marian prior to Parker's arrival in the village, and yet Marian had sailed off into the sunset with Parker, leaving that decision to Archer and Bentley – and leaving Stella worrying Marian might soon regret her hasty choices. Thankfully, it appeared Marian had no regrets at all … so far. Parker was the love of Marian's life. Stella sincerely hoped it would stay that way.

If anything, Marian's postcard made it clear that she and Parker were even more in love now than they had been when they had sailed away.

Ah, young love. The thrill of it. The excitement. The sacrifices it made you willing to make. The way it made any situation seem perfect if it allowed you to spend time with the one you loved.

Even at seventy-five, Stella could remember how that felt.

And Marian deserved True Love.

But then again, didn't everybody?

Stella breathed out a long, wistful sigh. For some people, that just wasn't meant to be. No matter how hard they tried. No matter what they were prepared to give up. No matter how many lonely nights they spent asking themselves, 'What if...?'

Perhaps if they ... if she ... had made different choices...

No. She mustn't let her mind wander down that path. Only painful memories waited for her there. No point in looking back. She had learnt that over the years. No use in wondering what might have been.

Only madness lay that way.

And yet, her heart had fluttered just a little when she had first seen the postcard and that momentary flicker of ... anticipation ... hope ... whatever it had been, almost took her breath away. Which was more than a little annoying.

Stella tutted and mentally rebuked herself.

He had made his choices and she had made hers. She had to live with that knowledge. She had lived with it... for almost fifty-five years.

Had it really been that long? Where had that time gone? It had been a lifetime ago, and yet, at moments like today, it felt as if it had only been yesterday. Once, oh so long ago now, she had been as deeply in love with someone as Marian was with Parker.

Stella tutted loudly again and shook her head, glancing at the postcard. The image of the French Riviera had brought it all back. Not that the memory of that idyllic year was ever really very far away. Stella tried not to think of it too often. Over the years she had whittled it down to maybe ... once every few months or so. Or when something about the French Riviera popped up on TV, or anything to do with olives, lemons, or lavender. Which was one of the reasons she didn't watch much TV.

It was ridiculous, after all these years, to have retained such vivid memories, to still harbour even an ounce of hope, but this wasn't the only time she had experienced such twinges recently, or asked herself those difficult questions. She would be doing that until she took her last breath, and there was nothing she could do about it. No matter how deeply she tried to keep her feelings buried.

What harm was it doing anyway? No one was getting hurt – apart from herself, maybe. And the memories weren't really painful now. They hadn't been for a long time.

She wasn't sure precisely when her heart had stopped hurting when she thought of him. Of the fields of lavender swaying gently in the breeze; the scent seeping into her skin, mingled with the citrus aroma of the lemons growing year-round on the trees, and the woody fragrance of the olive groves. Of the hours they had laboured; their feelings for one another growing as each crop ripened and was harvested. Of snatched kisses under skies of the brightest blue; of swimming naked in warm, azure waters sheltered by rocky cliffs; of making love on sultry, summer nights, and making promises in the warm winds of autumn. Of clinging to each other during the rains and storms. Of the misery and heartbreak of that final goodbye.

Oh, all right. Maybe her heart still ached – just a tiny bit – whenever she thought of him.

But it wasn't just the postcard that had brought these memories to the fore after so many years.

She blamed *that* on Stanley Talbot.

Stella could not recall how long Stanley had lived in the village, nor when he had first arrived in Clementine Cove, but he had lived there for several years. She, like most of the other residents, had found him pleasant enough at first, and he was welcomed with open arms, but there was something about him that made Stella feel uneasy in his company. And she wasn't the only one who began to feel that way. Her friend Rosie Parker, sister of the local vicar, told her she was being ridiculous and should give the man a chance. But then Stella was fairly certain Rosie would like to give Stanley Talbot a lot more than 'a chance'. It was clear to Stella, if not to everyone else that Rosie had a soft spot for Stanley. For a while it seemed the feeling might be mutual but nothing came of it and instead of blushing whenever Stanley appeared, Rosie began to look somewhat annoyed and Stella wondered, more than once, if Stanley had spurned Rosie's advances.

Stella never did find out because Rosie refused to discuss it and Stanley never told anyone anything. Ever. He kept his cards close to his chest, and yet he was overly keen to discuss other people's comings and goings. Stella often caught him watching people, or eavesdropping on conversations.

He always asked everyone a great many questions, and he constantly jotted in the notebook he took everywhere with him, or snapped photos of unsuspecting people with his phone camera.

Stanley gave Stella the creeps the more she got to know him over the years. Not that anyone really knew him. But his true colours came to light just last Christmas Eve, shortly after he died, when several of the villagers received a message from beyond the grave. Or to be precise, via a parcel courier, along with a beautifully wrapped gift and a note containing Stanley's best wishes and apologies for the way he had behaved. The note was written on a card attached to the gift and it read: "With the compliments of the season and good wishes for a Happy New Year from Stanley Talbot."

The gift itself turned out to be a file – a file that held the recipient's deeply hidden secrets.

It seemed Stanley Talbot knew them all. Or at least he thought he did.

Thankfully for Stella, Stanley did not know all of hers, but it had made her remember things she had spent a lifetime trying to forget.

Only later did everyone discover that the files had been sent by a woman with whom Stanley had been in love. And he had changed his ways because of her. His intentions had definitely not been honourable when he had spent his time compiling those files, but falling in love had made him see the error of his ways. The files were sent out to those named on each file tab, as per his final request, as his way of making amends.

Stella's secrets were hardly mind-blowing, unlike some others, she suspected – apart from one. But luckily for her that seemed to be the one thing Stanley had *not* known about her.

And in reality, these days, her secret would not seem so bad. Except to those who thought of her as Stella Pinkheart, the prim and proper, retired school teacher, the do-gooder who would not say 'Boo' to a goose. The woman who believed the words, please and thank you were compulsory; who maintained that people should know right from wrong; that one should do unto others as they would be done by. The grey-haired, slightly frail-looking elderly spinster who lived a quiet, almost reclusive life and eked out her now meagre (thanks to the ever-spiralling-upwards cost of living) pension.

Everyone knew that looks could be deceiving, but what would all those people say if they discovered she had once thrown caution to the wind and had fallen in love with a married man? And not just fallen in love with him; they had had a passionate affair. She had been prepared to sacrifice everything for him. Everything. And she would have done so willingly.

If only he had let her.

Her life did not turn out as she had once expected. She survived the heartbreak, much to her surprise, and eventually packed away her dreams and learnt how to cope without love.

Her mother insisted they put the 'entire sordid episode' behind them. Her father said later that it was the making of her. And in a way, it was. Stella went back to college, and then to university. She gained an English degree and went on to become a teacher, just like her own parents. And she had loved her years teaching.

She loved living in Clementine Cove. And she loved taking care of Marian and helping to guide Marian's journey into adulthood. Not that she loved the fact that her own best friends, Marian's beloved mother and father, had died, leaving Stella as Marian's guardian. Stella still missed them both so much. But she had buried her own sadness and devoted herself to Marian, doing everything she could to make the then teenager's life as happy as it could be after the poor darling had lost first one and then the other of her beloved parents.

Losing the Blythes had been traumatic – more so for their only daughter than it had for Stella, naturally, but that had ultimately brought Stella unexpected happiness. Not having children of her own was one of Stella's biggest regrets. Looking after Marian had helped to fill the void. And yet she had often felt guilty for gaining that happiness at the expense of her two dearest friends.

Now Marian was thousands of miles away too. But she was blissfully happy and that meant Stella was happy for her. Even if she did feel a little lonely and lost without Marian's lovely face and smile to brighten up her days.

Marian had tried to persuade Stella to get a smart phone, or some software on her computer so that they could keep in touch by video calls, but at seventy-five, Stella was too old to learn all of that modern technology, and secretly, she had no wish to open what she considered to be a can of worms. People were often telling her that they had found a long-lost friend on some social networking site or other.

'All you have to do is look,' she had heard people say. 'It's so easy to learn how to do it.'

But Stella didn't want to look. She was too afraid of what she might find.

And besides, it might be easy for some people to learn how to use all this new-fangled gadgetry, but these days everything she tried to take in seemed to seep right back out again.

She did have a mobile phone – and one that doubled as a small tablet (not that Stella really understood how or why) but her friend Rosie constantly laughed at her when Stella used it.

'Didn't they use those on the Ark?' Rosie would say, sniggering at her own joke. Or, 'The Ten Commandments were written on tablets just like that one.'

Most of Rosie's quips had a biblical connotation, no doubt due to the fact that Rosie's brother was the Reverend Wilfred Parker, vicar of St Mary's in the Wood. Both Rosie and Will, as the vicar was known, were unmarried and they lived together in Rosehip Cottage, an exceedingly pretty building nestled behind the church. Mind you, all of the cottages in Clementine Cove were picturesque. Apart from the new-builds on the housing estate at the edge of the village. Not that they were all that new now. Neither were they unattractive. But they weren't as quaint as the original cottages, that much everyone did agree with. The estate had shot up more than ten years ago, despite vociferous objections from Rosie and some of the other locals. Rosie referred to the occupants of those homes as, 'The Great Unwashed' and she and Stella had almost come to blows over that on several occasions.

'You can't refer to people as "The Great Unwashed!" Stella was stunned when Rosie first used the term.

'I can and I shall,' Rosie replied.

'It's demeaning.'

'So what?'

'It's also unkind.'

Rosie smirked. 'I don't think anyone has ever accused me of being overly kind.'

'Rosamunde Parker!' Stella used people's full names when she was annoyed with them, and Rosie's name was Rosamunde. 'That's not something to be proud of. Especially not from someone who is the vicar's sister.'

'I'm his sister, not his wife. Will has his life and I have mine.'

There was no point in talking to Rosie when she was in 'one of her moods', but the odd thing was, Rosie loved her brother dearly and frequently helped him with his duties, both in and out of the church. She also often introduced herself as 'the vicar's sister', and it was a role she clearly enjoyed.

It was as if Rosie were two different people sometimes. One minute she could be the dutiful sister of the handsome, kind and generous vicar, the next she could be tearing a strip or two off some unsuspecting person who unfortunately happened cross her path when she was in one of her moods. More often than not, that person was Stella. She and Rosie might be friends, but they certainly were not close, either in age or in temperament. In truth, Stella was not sure she actually liked Rosie very much at all. If she had, surely she wouldn't have made up the nickname, Nosy Parker, for Rosie. And Stella was fairly certain that Rosie felt the same way about her. She could only imagine what names Rosie used for her, behind her back.

    Stella shot a look at the grandfather clock in her hall, its chimes ringing out that it was noon. It had belonged to her parents and had, for many years, run a little late, just as she was, today. She placed the pile of post on the shelf of the radiator cover near the front door, but kept hold of Marian's postcard, which she slipped into her handbag that was sitting on the bottom step of her stairs. She took her raincoat from one of the hooks on the ornate wooden coat stand and buttoned it up despite the bright, early May sunshine beaming in through the windows. The forecast said there was a wind chill today and Stella felt the cold more these days than she used to.

Now she must rush. She was meeting Rosie for lunch at The Bow and Quiver, and Rosie despised tardiness, much as Stella did herself. Luckily, Pinkheart Cottage, the pale pink painted, thatched cottage which had been in her family since it was built back in the early 1800s was a mere stone's throw from the pub and it would take her a matter of minutes to reach her destination. Hopefully, Rosie would be in a good mood and wouldn't comment on Stella being late. She usually was when she had gossip to share, and she had told Stella on the phone that morning that she had heard a particularly interesting piece of news.

Chapter 2

Rosie Parker sat at a table in the window of The Bow and Quiver and stared out at the old lighthouse on the rock just a few metres away from the rugged coastline of Arrow Point where the pub was situated. There was movement in one of The Lighthouse windows; Rosie could make out the shape of a tall, slim male ... or perhaps a tall, slim female with extremely short hair.

She didn't really care. Tourists didn't particularly concern her – unless they behaved in an unseemly manner in which case she had something to say about it. And frequently did.

She would quite like to know how much the current owners, Cordelia and Charles King made from renting the place out though, but they kept a tight lid on their financial details. As tight as the grip they both kept on their wallets.

The Kings were not on Rosie's list of those she called her friends. Few people were. Her list was incredibly short. So short that it wasn't even a list. Her friends consisted of her brother, Will, Stella Pinkheart … and … Stanley Talbot. But he was dead so he no longer counted. And in truth, he wasn't as good a friend as she had thought. That became clear at Christmas, after his death. Although long before that, Stanley had started giving her the cold shoulder. Whenever she asked him if he fancied a drink after choir practice, he always had other plans. Or when she popped round to see him having made up some excuse or other for her visit, he told her he was in the middle of something and didn't have time to stop, or he was just on his way out. Eventually, she got the message: Stanley Talbot wasn't interested in her.

But she didn't want to think about Stanley right now. Or ever again for that matter. Nor did she want to dwell on the realisation that she only had two friends, one of whom was her brother. How depressing was that?

There were lots of people she chatted to, especially in her role of the vicar's sister, but none of them were her friends. She couldn't call them up and tell them her troubles. Not that she would, even if she could. Rosie didn't like people knowing too much about her. She had never been one to 'share'. She enjoyed gossiping about others, but the thought of others gossiping about her sent shivers of revulsion down her spine. She was very careful to keep her secrets, hopes and dreams to herself. Although Stanley had known far more of them than she had imagined was possible.

She watched as two more people walked up the path to the door of The Lighthouse, as the place was unimaginatively named. One was definitely a woman and the other was a little girl. Rosie couldn't tell the child's age from this distance but the golden-haired youngster was probably around five or six, judging by her size and the way she skipped towards the steps while holding the woman's hand.

Rosie experienced a sudden stabbing pain in her chest. It felt as if the pink ribbon in the little girl's hair had stolen inside Rosie's body and wrapped itself into a knot around her heart. The pain was only fleeting but it had taken her by surprise and she sucked in a long, deep breath in order to regain her equilibrium. She wasn't sure why that had happened and for a moment it unnerved her, but she quickly dismissed the feeling. It must have been something she had eaten; although it was at least five hours since she and Will had eaten breakfast. She straightened her back and continued to observe the woman and the child, who were met at the door by the person Rosie had seen previously. The tall, slim man lifted the child in his arms and swung her inside. Rosie thought she could hear the gurgles of laughter, but it was probably only the wind rustling through the trees close to the pub.

The Lighthouse was a popular holiday rental, especially as the light still functioned, albeit on an automatic timer, but it seemed an odd place to bring a child. There was no garden to speak of, just a tiny patch of grass and a concrete patio on which sat a driftwood table with two wooden bench seats either side. A gravel path led down to a small inlet with a sliver of sandy beach and a tiny wooden jetty where the row boat that came with the rental property, bobbed on the gently lapping waves.

Strictly speaking, the boat was only necessary during exceptionally high tides. Most of the time it was possible to walk from the inlet, over a bank of sand and rocks to the shingle beach at the foot of the rocky promontory of Arrow Point. It was a distance of around fifteen metres and took less than five minutes to cross. But at certain times this rocky sandbank was covered by water to a depth of up to a metre. Many holidaymakers said that rowing to The Lighthouse added to the experience, and the boat was popular with guests who liked to fish.

Rosie hoped these particular visitors had securely tied the rope. One summer, a few years ago, the boat came loose and drifted out to sea. Rosie smiled at the memory. Cordelia King had not been happy. Neither had the couple who were staying at The Lighthouse for their honeymoon. The Kings had retained the hefty deposit by way of compensation. Although Charles had also claimed for the loss of the boat via his insurance. Stanley had told Rosie that. And amazingly, the insurance company had paid up.

Rosie couldn't fathom why anyone would want to spend their honeymoon on a rock, in a building with more stairs than floor space, and no room service. But the interior décor was equivalent to any five-star hotel, and the place was booked week in, week out throughout the year, and mainly by young couples. Cordelia often boasted about the rave reviews it received.

Rosie had once been tempted to find a way to leave a bad review, but her position as the Reverend Parker's sister had, on that occasion, got the better of her and she had refrained from doing so. Still … maybe one day.

Being Will's sister had stopped her from doing a great many things over the years. But ten years ago, when she reached her fortieth birthday and was still undeniably single, and living with her brother in the rectory, Rosehip Cottage, she made a monumental decision. She would, of course, continue to support him in every way she could; she'd play the role she had mastered as the dutiful, spinster sister of the village vicar, but she would also live her own life and do the things she wanted to do. She wouldn't tell Will, though. He was a lovely man and she adored him, but he did have a tendency to lecture and he was a bit of a goody two-shoes. Not a bad trait for a vicar, but not thrilling to be around day in, day out. Especially for Rosie, who had a bit of a rebellious streak. Something she definitely tried to keep under wraps.

Not that she was unhappy living with Will. They jogged along together rather nicely, and they actually ran together almost every day. Running was something they both enjoyed and it helped them both stay fit. Will's hair had gone grey years ago and so had Rosie's, but unlike Will, she coloured hers. She was tall and slim and looked stunning in her tight-fitting lycra which made her, currently red, hair stand out. She made a striking impression and few people would guess that she was fifty, apart from those who had known her all her life. And that was a large proportion of the population of Clementine Cove.

Unbeknown to Will, Rosie had acquired several vices. Luckily, she was very good at keeping secrets. She had been doing that for the last ten years. Will would have a fit if he discovered how she spent her time when she wasn't helping him. She had become an online gambler. And gambling wasn't her only vice.

Sometimes she wondered if she might have had a different life. She had envisaged that with Stanley Talbot but boy, had she got him wrong. His Christmas gift came as a shock to her as much as it had to everyone else. It was bad enough that he seemed to know all of her secrets; it was even worse that he knew that she had been in love with him.

The door of the pub swung open and Rosie spotted Stella. Rosie tapped the face of her expensive, jewel encrusted watch with one bright red painted fingernail. She had bought it from the proceeds of her latest online win. It was a rather substantial amount and she smirked at the look on Stella's face.

'Am I late?' Stella asked, joining Rosie at the table and pulling out the chair opposite.

'Yes,' said Rosie. 'What kept you?'

Stella tutted. 'Two minutes, if that. Is that a new watch?'

Rosie smiled and twisted her wrist back and forth, the jewels glinting in the rays of sunlight streaming through the windows.

'Five minutes. And yes.'

'It looks expensive. Or is it fake?'

Rosie raised perfectly shaped brows. 'Fake? Are you being serious? Of course it's not. I've wanted this watch since I saw it advertised in a magazine.'

'Clearly not the local parish magazine.' Stella grinned at her.

'*Cosmo*, I believe. Or perhaps it was in *Country Life*.' Rosie grinned back and waved her hand nonchalantly in the air. 'It doesn't matter. What are you looking so pleased about?'

Stella's smile grew wider. 'I've had a postcard from Marian.' She dived her hand into her handbag and rummaged around before holding up a slightly bent postcard in front of Rosie.

Rosie took it, read it and tossed it back across the table.

'I still can't believe you didn't try to talk her out of going off with a man she hardly knew, but it sounds as if she's having fun. She always struck me as an odd little thing, and everyone was convinced she held a torch for Archer. I suppose Elodie's arrival put paid to that and Marian grabbed hold of the first man who crossed her path.'

'Odd!' Stella said, her voice a shrill squawk. 'There is nothing odd about my darling Marian, and don't you dare say there is. If anyone is odd, it's you, Rosamunde Parker.'

'Oh don't get all huffy with me, Stella. I didn't mean anything by it.'

Stella narrowed her eyes. 'I should hope not. I'm not getting huffy. I'm merely stating facts. And I know for a fact that Marian might have had a crush on Archer when they were younger, but she fell in love with Parker the moment they first met. She told me so herself.'

'I'm sure she did. I wish them a long and happy life together. But I don't want to talk about Marian.' Rosie glanced around to see if anyone was within earshot but the pub restaurant where they sat, was virtually empty, for a change. 'Have you heard the news about Archer?'

Stella's gaze shot towards the bar where Archer was serving a group of men and laughing cordially.

'Shush, Rosie. He's only over there.'

'He can't hear me from there. You can't hear what they're saying, can you?'

Stella shook her head. 'No.'

'So he can't hear what we're saying.' She leant forward a fraction closer to Stella nonetheless. 'I was out running this morning, with Will, as usual. His laces came untied just as we reached Marian's café. Or what was her café. Have you seen it lately? Almost unrecognisable. If it weren't for the fact that I adore Bentley's food, I might have to have a word with the planning department, but that's another matter. I happened to overhear a conversation between Iris and Bentley. What is going on between those two? Do you know? One minute they're a couple, the next they're not. I can't keep up with it. Well, that's neither here nor there either. I heard Iris ask how Bentley would cope when Archer left for Australia.'

Stella blinked at her. 'That's hardly news. We've all been wondering about that.'

'Yes. But we all thought Archer was going to Aus in July.'

Stella furrowed her brows. 'And...?'

Rosie beamed triumphantly. 'And Iris said, "when Archer leaves ... next week". Next week, Stella. Not July.'

'So ... he and Elodie are leaving earlier than planned. Again, that's hardly thrilling.'

The smile slid from Rosie's face. 'Well, there must be a reason they've changed their plans, mustn't there? I thought we should come here and find out.'

Stella sighed. 'I wondered why you offered to treat me to lunch.'

'It's not the first time I've treated you to lunch, but I thought it might be better coming from you. If I ask, he'll think I'm being nosy. You can tell him that Marian was asking how he and Elodie were and then you can find a way to wheedle it out of him.'

Rosie was certain Stella would want to know just as much as she did, but sometimes the woman had to be convinced.

'Rosie! "Wheedle it out of them"! What do you think I am, exactly? I will ask, but if Archer or Elodie are not forthcoming, I will leave it at that.'

Chapter 3

Iris Talbot perched on the window seat in her bedroom, one of the many window seats in Clementine Cottage, and sipped from the large mug of coffee that Bentley had made her before he had jumped in the shower. She listened to the water cascading over his body and sighed.

What was wrong with her? She had only known the guy since Christmas and the excitement was already wearing off. In truth, it had been for a while. Why wasn't she dashing to the shower, jumping in beside him, and having incredible sex? Because sex with Bentley was incredible. That much she was sure of. But it seemed that once, or maybe twice a night was enough for her these days. And that was something she never expected to say. Although the only person she would say that to was Elodie, her dearest friend.

She sighed louder and longer. Soon she wouldn't be able to say that to El. Or say anything at all. Okay, they would still chat on the phone, or via FaceTime or whatever, but that was hardly the same thing, was it? El had only told Iris the other day that she and Archer would be off to Aus much sooner than they had originally planned, but Iris was already missing her best friend. And they were not leaving until next week.

Why did things always have to change? She and El had only come to Clementine Cove for a long weekend before Christmas and now they both lived here full time. They had both been unattached when they first came; now El was living with Archer in his pub, and Iris was dating Bentley ... on and off. That was change enough, as far as Iris was concerned.

But nope. Now El was going to the other side of the planet, and God alone knew for how long. El had planned to visit her sister in Melbourne for a few weeks in the summer, but as soon as Archer discovered his long-lost daughter lived there too, not only had El and Archer decided to go together, they'd also agreed the visit should be extended. They had talked about going soon after Christmas, but there was so much other stuff going on that they both felt they needed time to let all the changes sink in, so they'd agreed to go in July. Now it was being brought forward. And why? All because of Iris' bloody, Uncle Stanley. Although to be fair, if it hadn't been for Stanley, Archer wouldn't have known where his daughter was in the first place.

But for a dead guy, Stanley was causing an awful lot of trouble. Mind you, he had done that all his life, according to Iris' parents. Even so, surely telling Archer the whereabouts of his own daughter was enough? Why had the bloody man had to tell the damn daughter where to find her dad? Honestly. Did no one believe in keeping secrets anymore?

Elizabeth, the daughter, had written to Archer, and as a result, they'd talked once on the phone, and suddenly, everything had to change. And all because of Stanley's bloody files.

Although technically, of course, it wasn't Stanley who had sent his files out to everyone; it was the love of his life, Hermione Dunmore, who had done that. And she had said she hadn't read any of them, so she probably didn't know that the young woman named Elizabeth, in Melbourne, was the daughter Archer Rhodes had been searching for his entire, adult life. Maybe if she had, Hermione wouldn't have sent that particular file. Or perhaps she would. Who knew what made people tick?

In theory, Bentley should have made Iris tick. On paper, he was her dream guy. A gorgeous, blond-haired hunk who worked as a chef at The Bow and Quiver. Not just good looking and good in bed, the man also excelled in the kitchen. What more could she possibly want? He was clever, funny, caring and kind. He was the perfect guy. And yet, other than the first few times she had looked at him, there simply wasn't that ... spark. Her insides didn't turn to mush when he smiled at her, or brushed her hand with his. He may be the perfect guy. But he wasn't the perfect guy for *her*.

Did such a guy even exist?

She had had her fair share of relationships. And one or two hook ups that were merely about sex and nothing else. None of them had lasted and none of them had made her think, 'This is The One'.

Elodie had told her that the moment El saw Archer, she knew. And Archer said he felt the same about El. Would Iris ever have that feeling?

Did she want to?

She was the wrong side of thirty-five but forty was years away. She had plenty of time to find The One. If such a being existed for her.

Didn't she?

Perhaps she ought to start looking before too long.

But then again … Bentley was fun to be with. His food was to die for, that much was certain. And right now, she would kill for the man's Eggs Benedict.

And maybe, a little bit of sex on the side. After all, it was a shame to let that body go to waste, and it had been at least seven hours since Iris had last had sex. Not that she was counting.

Chapter 4

Stella opened her front door and stepped inside, a sudden feeling of loneliness sweeping over her. It happened from time to time and she had been getting used to it, but it was becoming more frequent now. It made her sad to think that, once that front door was closed it could often be days until she spoke to someone face to face again. She used to be able to go and see Marian in Cove Café every day if she wanted to, but now Marian had gone, and so too had the café ... for now. At least that was one bit of news that Stella had managed to get out of Archer. But not the news Rosie – and she – had set out to obtain.

'I've had a postcard from Marian,' Stella had told Archer when he came to take their lunch orders.

'That's good,' he replied before she had time to say more. 'I had a video call with her last night. She's really caught the sun and looks the best I've seen her in years. The Med obviously agrees with her, and life aboard *The Dream* is even better than she had hoped.' He beamed at Stella. 'And I think we both know she had very high hopes. But I suppose she told you how fantastic things are, on her postcard. Parker's a great guy. I liked him from the start. Elodie says Marian and Parker were made for one another. It's funny how things work out, isn't it? Anyway. What can I get you two lovely ladies? But wait. Before I forget, I know you'll be pleased to hear that Cove Café will be reopening next week. Marian said she'd like to be here, but of course, she can't. I gave her a video tour of the place and she's delighted with the result, which is good. And such a relief. Not that I was worried. We'd discussed our plans in detail before she left and we've been in touch every few days since then, so there weren't really any surprises.'

'Have you found someone to run the café?' Rosie interrupted.

'Yep. Her name's Harley. She's just obtained a diploma in culinary arts and is looking for an entry level job in the food industry, so running a café will be as good a place as any to start. She's the daughter of a friend and she lives just a few minutes away from the café, so she's perfect in more ways than one.'

'Harley? Do we know her?' Rosie asked. 'I don't recall a Harley.'

Archer grinned. 'She lives on the new estate, Rosie, so no, you probably wouldn't. But she's a lovely girl, so give her a chance.'

Rosie's brows shot up at the mention of the estate but she managed to hide her distaste.

'Of course we shall, Archer. Why would you think otherwise?'

Archer smirked. 'Do you really want me to answer that?'

Stella stepped in. 'That's exciting news, Archer. You must be thrilled. And it's good to know that you'll have everything up and running long before you and Elodie set off on your vacation to Australia, isn't it?'

Archer's expression wavered towards excitement for a split second but then the calm and friendly smile returned.

'Yep. Everything will be under control. But it's not as if we'll be out of touch or anything. That's the wonderful thing about technology these days, Stella. You really ought to try it. I know Marian wanted you to. Maybe you should have a rethink. You could chat to her as often as you liked. Much better than waiting for a postcard, I promise you that.'

His comment had made Stella forget the reason she was there, although from his reply he wasn't going to divulge his change of plans to her and Rosie in any event. But it had made her think. She was thrilled to get a postcard. How much better would it be to see Marian face to face? Albeit via a screen.

'Perhaps you're right,' she said.

She made a mental note to spend an afternoon at Millside very soon. In addition to a couple of mobile phone shops, there was a store called *TechWiz*, or something like that. She hadn't really taken much notice of it before. The gadgetry in the window and the streams of teenagers dashing in and out assured her it wasn't a place she would find anything of interest to her. Perhaps it was time she stepped over the threshold. Assuming she could cope with the flashing lights, pounding music, and the cacophony of excited voices that emanated from the vast expanse of the store. Perhaps she'd go one day next week. Millside was always heaving with people on a Friday, and the weekends were even worse.

But she could not go on Monday. Cove Café was reopening on Monday at exactly 10 a.m. and Stella wanted to be one of the first customers to set foot inside. The Bistro wouldn't open until Thursday evening, but Stella wasn't particularly interested in that.

She rarely went out for an evening meal. At her age, anything she ate after 6 p.m. generally gave her indigestion. When she was younger, she loved going out to dinner, trying new dishes and drinking a little too much wine, but not now. These days she was happy eating tea at 5 p.m. and having the occasional treat of a chocolate digestive biscuit with her mug of Horlicks at 9.30 before she went to bed.

She did go out one evening a week, on Wednesday, but that was only to choir practice at the church. It was previously on Friday, but a few people complained and asked to change the day. Rosie said no, but Will said he could understand why Friday might not be the best evening for some.

'Because they would rather go to the pub,' Rosie grumbled.

'Because they would prefer to spend the evening with their families,' Will replied.

Stella, for once, agreed with Rosie, but the day was changed, nonetheless.

Other than choir practice, Stella spent her evenings at home, reading, sometimes watching TV, or if the weather was good, pottering in her garden. Being on her own hadn't bothered her that much before, but then Marian often popped in to say hello, or called her for a chat.

Stella closed her front door and turned the lock. The emptiness of her cottage enveloped her. What usually felt like a haven of comfort from the comings and goings of the world now felt like a prison. Stella was in solitary confinement, and would be until she opened her door and ventured out again. And that wouldn't be until she went to church on Sunday morning. Today was only Friday.

This definitely was not the life Stella had imagined she would be living.

Chapter 5

Rosie was disappointed that she and Stella had been unable to garner details of Archer and Elodie's changed plans. She liked to be at the forefront of village life, and the first to know all the latest news and the comings and goings of the residents. But there was still time. She had heard Iris tell Bentley that Archer and Elodie would be leaving next week. That meant she had the weekend. Perhaps she could persuade Will to join her for a drink in The Bow and Quiver on Saturday evening. Archer liked Will. Maybe her brother would succeed where Stella had so dismally failed.

Rosie had no idea what was going on with Stella these days. The woman seemed to be a shadow of her former self. It was probably something to do with Marian leaving, but why couldn't Stella just get over it? She had told Rosie that she was thrilled for Marian. And yet, whenever Rosie saw her, the woman looked downright miserable.

True, Stella seemed happier today, having received Marian's postcard, but the euphoria hadn't lasted long. Although Stella did now appear to be more inclined to consider embracing modern technology, so at least something positive had come from their lunch at the pub. Even if it wasn't Rosie obtaining some juicy gossip.

And now Will was late for their run. Today was clearly not her day. Nothing had gone right. The shower in her ensuite was playing up again and she had been sprayed with freezing water; then Will, who had promised to call a plumber, forgot to do so. Must she do everything herself? On top of that, Stella had let her down, a parcel had gone astray, old Jemima Judge, of Judge's Farm, had nodded off during evening prayers and snored her way through Will's entire sermon, and now he was late. What on earth was keeping him? He always closed the church at 6.30 on weekdays. When Rosie left to return to Rosehip Cottage to get changed, Will said he was right behind her.

Clearly he wasn't. And he hadn't returned to the cottage. She had called up the stairs to him at least three times, and when he hadn't responded to her fourth shout for him to 'get a move on', she had gone to his room and rapped on the door, opening it to check, when yet again, he hadn't answered.

She glanced at her watch for the umpteenth time. They always ran at 7.00 p.m. and it was now nearly ten minutes past.

More than a little annoyed, she ran to the church and rattled the wrought iron handle. The door was locked as she assumed it would be. The rectory, Rosehip Cottage sat opposite the church with no more than twenty metres or so between them, and that included the narrow lane only wide enough for one car at a time. So where had the man disappeared to?

'Will!' she exclaimed.

She spotted him just as she had taken her phone from her pocket after remembering their phones had apps to track one another. Not that either of them ever ventured far from Clementine Cove, at least, not without each other, so they really had no need for tracking apps – until now. She shoved her phone back in her pocket and called to him again.

'Will!'

He had his back to her, so either he couldn't hear her, or he had chosen to ignore her yells. But what was he doing at Sunnycliff Cottage? And deep in conversation with Penny Walsh.

Rosie's lip curled. Penny was Hermione Dunmore's sister. And Hermione was the widow with whom Stanley Talbot had fallen madly in love. And not only that; for whom he had totally transformed his ways. Rosie was not a fan of Hermione's and consequently, nor was she a fan of Penny's. Although Rosie had never particularly liked Penny, even before Hermione came on the scene.

Penny was around the same age as Rosie, but looked several years younger, even without make up. Reason enough to dislike her. On top of that, Penny had some very odd ways. She was a self-confessed pagan, for one. For another, she eschewed modern medicine relying instead on ancient herbal remedies. She read tea leaves and tarot cards. Made creams, and soaps, and candles. Took in strays, both animal and human. And annoyingly, never had a bad word to say about anyone. Like Rosie, Penny was single, but she openly admitted to having lived with a man in the past. Rosie was more than a little envious of that. Living in sin, some of the parishioners might have called it, but Rosie, and even Will, were modern, understanding and forgiving. Well, Will was understanding and forgiving. Rosie, not so much.

Rosie glanced at her watch again. She had told Stella that she had seen it in a magazine; the truth was, she had seen it on Hermione Dunmore's wrist at Stanley Talbot's funeral on Christmas Eve, and had searched for it, or something similar, via her laptop. One of the results was an advert – in a magazine. So that wasn't a total lie. But when Rosie finally tracked down the watch, she was astonished by the price. It was a few months until her online gambling finally produced a substantial win, large enough for her to buy it. Right now though, even the cheapest watch would've shown the same time – 7.20 p.m. ... and Will was still standing on the front path of Sunnycliff Cottage chatting with Penny Walsh as if he had completely forgotten that he was keeping his sister waiting.

Rosie pulled out her phone once more and this time she sent him a text. It said, 'You're clearly busy with Penny Walsh. I'm going running without you.'

Chapter 6

Iris was feeling sorry for herself as she left The Bow and Quiver and headed towards Clementine Cottage. It was 10 p.m. on a Friday night and she was going home – alone. When had life become so exciting?

'When you moved to Clementine Cove,' she told herself, sneering.

She had spent most of the evening helping Elodie decide what to take, and what not to take, to Australia. Although Elodie told her she wasn't being helpful at all.

'Anyone would think you don't want me to go on this trip,' Elodie said, when Iris vetoed yet another dress. 'At this rate I won't have anything to wear when I get off the plane.'

Iris topped up their wine glasses and shrugged. 'They'd be right. I don't want you to go. No that's not true. Of course I want you to go. I just don't want you to stay away for so long. A month was going to be bad enough. Three months is a lifetime. And now you're saying it might be longer. Nope. I won't allow it. I'll miss you far too much. What am I supposed to do without you here?'

'Aww! I'll miss you too.' Elodie dropped the dress she was holding, onto the bed where Iris was sitting cross-legged, and pulled Iris into a hug. 'But we'll chat, text and FaceTime every day. Although maybe not all three on the same day.' Elodie eased Iris away and looked her directly in the eye. 'And the time will fly. You know that. I mean, doesn't it feel like only yesterday that we arrived in Clementine Cove?'

Iris couldn't argue with that. They had arrived just before Christmas, planning to stay for a long weekend. It definitely didn't feel as though they had now been living in the village for more than four months.

Iris shrugged again. 'I suppose so. I'm still not happy though. And I'm going to be so lonely. I may have to go back to London and stay with Mum and Dad for a while. Or ask them to come down here.'

Elodie laughed. 'You won't be lonely. You've got Bentley, for one thing.'

'And we all know what that one thing is,' Iris interrupted, comically raising and lowering her eyebrows.

Elodie laughed louder. 'And you've still got your sense of humour. Seriously though. You know lots of people in the village.'

'But they're not my friends. And with Marian gone, other than Bentley, I'm not sure there's anyone else in their thirties.'

'Of course there are.'

'Oh yeah? Name one.'

'There's … Er. Oh okay. I can't think of anyone right now. But there are. There must be. I'll ask Archer. He'll know.' Elodie's face lit up. 'Hey! I'll get him to introduce you to some of them before we leave.'

'Hmm. Before next week? Good luck with that. I'm hungry.' Iris changed the subject. 'Are you hungry?'

'I could eat. Let's go and see what your boyfriend has to offer. I can finish this later. I'll probably get a lot more done without you here.'

'Oy!' Iris tried to look offended but Elodie just laughed and linked arms with her.

'You know it's true,' Elodie said.

'Okay. Fair enough. But not the bit about Bentley being my boyfriend.'

They'd gone downstairs to the restaurant and despite the place being packed, a table had just become vacant.

'Perfect timing,' Archer said. 'But I thought you two were packing.'

'We were,' Iris confirmed. 'But El couldn't decide what to pack and what to leave, and I can only take so much indecision.'

Archer grinned. 'Yeah. I'm not sure I believe that.' He gave Elodie a quick kiss, winked at both of them, and went back to the bar to serve more customers.

'This might be our last meal together,' Iris said, once they were seated.

'Oh, don't be so dramatic.' Elodie playfully slapped Iris' hand. 'And besides, it won't be. You're joining us for Sunday lunch.'

'Oooh. Sunday lunch! I'd forgotten about that. That might be our last ... Okay. I won't say it.' Iris saw the expression on Elodie's face. 'But it might be.'

'No. It won't.' Elodie was emphatic. 'I'll make you a promise right now. We'll have breakfast together on the day I leave.'

'Oooh. Breakfast. I can taste the Eggs Benedict now.'

Iris knew she was being childish. Probably even a little selfish. But she couldn't help it. As much as they might joke about it, she really would miss Elodie. The longest they had been apart since they had first met at the age of five, was a few weeks at most. One month, she could cope with. Two, or three, or more months – well, she wasn't sure about that. Nevertheless, before she left the pub, she reassured her best friend that she wanted El and Archer to have a fabulous time in Melbourne. And she added that she hoped Archer's daughter, Elizabeth, would be as wonderful as the girl had seemed during Archer and Elizabeth's conversations.

As Iris strolled along the beach, she wondered what it would be like for Archer to finally meet his daughter after nineteen years. Would they hug one another right away? Would they feel awkward with each other? Or would the bond between them be so strong that it would seem as if they had known one another for Elizabeth's entire life? Iris suspected it would be the latter, knowing Archer as she did. After all, the man had been searching for Elizabeth for most, if not all, those years. And Elizabeth now knew that, thanks to Iris', Uncle Stanley.

Iris' scream clearly frightened the shadowy figure in front of her almost as much as the person's sudden appearance had frightened Iris.

'Jesus!' a man's voice said, sounding as if his heart had jumped into his throat and was stuck there.

'Back off!' Iris warned, her own heart pounding in her chest so loud it was all she could hear. 'My boyfriend's right behind me. And I'm calling the police.'

'What? Why? I'm not going to harm you. I'm not a mugger, if that's what you're thinking.'

Iris peered into the darkness, trying to calm herself. Why didn't this bloody village have streetlights? Not that they would shine any light onto the beach even if it did.

'Who are you? And what're you doing on the beach at this time of night?'

The man stepped out of the shadows and, as if on cue, the full moon appeared from behind a bank of heavy cloud, casting a beam of moonlight directly onto him.

Iris gasped. He was tall, slim and gorgeous. His only fault being that his hair appeared to be chestnut brown, not the blond hair that Iris required her ideal man to have.

'I might ask you the same thing,' he said, his voice now far more mellow, with just a slight edge.

And possibly the hint of a Scottish accent. Or was it Irish? Or American?

Why couldn't she tell? She was a voice coach. She could detect an accent from a mile off and pin point it almost exactly. Usually.

She met the curious look in his dark eyes. 'I'm Iris. I live here. I was walking home before you terrified the life out of me. And you are...?'

A smile crept across his generous mouth. 'I'm pleased to meet you, Iris. I'm Scott. Scott Fitzgerald. No relation to the famous American author who died in the 1940s. Although I am an author. Sadly not as famous. And I use a pen name to avoid the obvious comments I'd get if I didn't. My mother was a fan of the original F. Scott Fitzgerald. She thought it would be fun to name me after him. It isn't. Although she did omit the 'F', so that's something I should be thankful for. I'm here on holiday. A working holiday. I'm on a deadline. Which I'm going to miss the way things are going. I came out for a walk along the beach to clear my head. I'm staying at The Lighthouse with ... It seems I can't stop talking. Please say something. Anything.'

Iris burst out laughing. 'It's lovely to meet you, Scott Fitzgerald. It's a shame my name is Iris and not Daisy.'

'Daisy?' He seemed confused but laughed suddenly. 'Oh. Very good. The Daisy from his most famous novel, *The Great Gatsby*. Yes. That is a shame. But I can call you Daisy if you like.'

'Okay. What's your pseudonym? Please don't tell me it's something Gatsby.'

'How did you guess?' His laugh was melodic. He shook his head and his hair danced around his forehead. He ran his hand through it and pushed it back from his face, the laughter fading as he did so and the smile being replaced with a more serious and slightly sad expression. 'No. It's Scott North.'

Iris frowned. 'Scott North? Oh. For some reason I was expecting something a little more ... appealing? Sexy? I don't know. I hope you won't mind me saying so but it's not very ... imaginative, is it? What's your genre?'

'I write thrillers and crime fiction. And North was my wife's maiden name. So to me, it's both sexy and appealing. But I can see why it wouldn't be so for anyone else.'

'You're married? I mean ... I'm sorry. Scott North is a perfectly good name. Ignore me. I always say the wrong thing.'

Why did he have to be married? But wait. He hadn't mentioned a wife. He had mentioned a deadline. Perhaps he was here without her and she was back at home. Wherever that might be. Damn. Iris didn't date married men. Or hook up with them. She had done once, and that was one time too many. Why did this guy have to be so gorgeous? Although he wasn't her type anyway. He had the wrong hair colour. So why did she suddenly feel so deflated, just when things had been looking up?

'There's no need to apologise. You didn't know.' He took a deep breath and ran his hand through his hair once more. 'My wife died four years ago. When Ava, our daughter, was one.'

'Oh dear God! I'm so, so sorry. That must be … hard for you both.'

She had no idea what to say. First he had a wife and then no wife, but he did have a daughter. A five-year-old daughter. Nope. Iris couldn't go there. Kids were not her thing.

'Thanks. Yes. It's hard. But Ava doesn't remember her mum. I think that's good in a way, but it's also not. I want her to know about Veronica. I want her to know how wonderful she was.' He shrugged. 'I talk to Ava about her mum as much as I can without it becoming too maudlin.'

'Where is she now? Ava, I mean, not … well, you know.' Iris tutted under her breath. Yep. She was hopeless at this.

Surprisingly, he grinned. 'I hope Veronica is somewhere nice. I like to think she is. Ava, on the other hand, is with me. Which I hope is also nice. With me and my nanny. Not my nanny. My daughter's nanny. Although I suppose she works for me so … Anyway. She's a family friend. Veronica's best friend, as it happens. Her name's Trisha. She lives near us in Notting Hill. She's not really a nanny by profession, but she recently lost her job and decided to take a break. Ava loves her so that's why we thought this might be nice. Until Trisha decides it time to find a new position. She's actually a trained ... and here I go again! I'm babbling like an idiot. And why do I keep saying 'nice'? More importantly, why can't I stop telling you everything about me, and my friends and family? Do you have some sort of mind probing skills, or something?'

'Yep. That's just one of my super powers. Wait till I unleash the rest.'

He tipped his head slightly to one side. 'I'm not sure whether to be scared or excited. Excited, I think. But a little bit scared too.'

'Scared is definitely the way to go. Just ask any of my previous boyfriends.'

'What about your current boyfriend?'

'I don't have one.'

'Oh? You said he was right behind you.'

'I also said I was calling the police. I thought you were about to mug me. I was trying to scare you off.'

'With a fictious boyfriend and a phone call? Really? And you expected that to work?'

'Hey. We work with what we've got.'

'So ... does that mean you're single?'

'I am. Yes.' Guilt sprang up from nowhere. 'But in the interests of honesty – and because you've told me everything about yourself apart from your shoe size, I have been seeing someone. On and off. Very recently. Since Christmas. But we're not actually dating, as such. It's just a sex thing. I mean... God. Now look who can't shut up!'

'A sex thing? Hmm. That sounds ... nice.' His voice was even sexier now. 'And I'm an eleven.'

Iris let out a sigh as a wave of something akin to electricity flooded her body.

'You bet you are,' she said, virtually swooning on the spot. 'Oh! Er. What?'

He grinned. 'My shoe size. I'm an eleven.'

'Ah.' She grinned. 'Well, I'm an eleven, too,' she said, in the most seductive voice she could muster. 'But I'm not talking about my shoes.'

His grin grew broader. 'Just on the off-chance that you might bump into a real mugger, may I walk you home ... Daisy?' There was laughter in his eyes, and a lot more than that.

'Daisy? Oh right. The book. Yes, Mr Fitzgerald. You may.'

Chapter 7

'You almost had sex with a complete stranger you met on the beach?' Elodie stopped sorting through her wardrobe and glared at Iris, who was once again, sitting cross-legged on Elodie and Archer's bed, in The Bow and Quiver. 'What is wrong with you?'

'Okay! Don't have a go at me. I was feeling emotional. And he was ... nice.' Iris smiled, momentarily remembering last night's conversation with Scott, until she saw the expression on Elodie's face. 'Plus he was bloody gorgeous. But I'm beginning to wish I hadn't told you.'

She took a gulp from one of the mugs of coffee that Archer had made them before he had gone downstairs to prepare the pub for opening.

'I'm definitely wishing you hadn't told me.' Elodie tutted and shook her head. 'What about Bentley? He's such a lovely guy. How could you do this to him, Iris? And did you think, even for a second, how it might affect Archer?'

'Archer? Why would me having sex with Scott affect Archer? Not that we did have sex, so I don't know what you're getting so upset about. I did say, "almost", and you clearly heard that, having thrown it back at me. But I damn well wish we had now. At least it would've made this telling off worth it.'

'Because we're about to leave the pub restaurant and the soon to be open Cove Café Bistro in Bentley's capable hands for the next three months or so. Only Bentley might not be quite so capable if he's dealing with a broken heart.'

'Ah. I see. Er … no. I didn't think about that. But I thought Archer's parents were looking after the pub?'

'The pub, yes. The pub restaurant, no. That's going to be Bentley's domain. Along with the Café Bistro.'

'Right. Got it. But I don't think Bentley's heart would break if I slept with someone else. He's known from the start that this was just a casual thing between us. That we weren't dating or anything. That we're not a couple. That we're nothing like you and Archer. So I honestly don't think it'll be a problem.'

'Really? Are you one hundred per cent certain about that?'

'Y-yes.' Iris was fairly sure; but not one hundred per cent certain. 'Take last night for example. After you and I had supper, I told Bentley that I wasn't in the mood for sex and I was going to have an early night. If we were a couple, he would have still come round and spent the night. But he didn't. He said that was fine, because he had a lot on his mind and needed to think a few things through, and he'd see me in the morning.' Iris beamed at Elodie.

'Which was just as well, considering you had taken some stranger home with you instead.'

'Don't keep calling Scott a stranger.'

'He is a stranger. You only met him last night.'

'True. But he didn't feel like a stranger.' Iris let out a meaningful sigh. 'That's why I had to come here first thing and tell you about him. Well, not first thing. I've been up since 6.a.m., but you'll be pleased to know that I waited until what I thought Archer would consider a reasonable hour.'

'How thoughtful.' Elodie grinned, but Iris could tell she was still a little cross. 'I thought you'd come because you wanted breakfast.'

Iris smiled. 'I wouldn't say no, if you're offering.'

'Fine.' Elodie closed her wardrobe door. 'But … be careful, Iris. You obviously like the guy you met last night. And I heard what you said about him not feeling like a stranger. The thing is though, he is. Don't throw away something good for someone you know nothing about. That's all I'm saying.'

'Er. You didn't know anything about Archer, and yet you fell in love with him almost at first sight, may I remind you?'

Elodie blinked several times before replying. 'Are you saying you've fallen in love with this guy?'

'No! I don't know. Maybe. Just a little. He's gorgeous, funny and incredibly sexy. But he's not my usual type. For one thing, he doesn't have blond hair. For another, he's tall and slim, not tall and hunky. And yet … I don't know. There was just something about him. Something about last night.' She laughed joyfully. 'And I think I know more about him and his life after spending two hours in his company than I do about Bentley after spending almost four months in his. I even know Scott's shoe size. I have no idea what Bentley's is.'

Elodie frowned. 'What on earth does shoe size have to do with anything?'

Iris waved a hand in the air. 'You had to be there. The point is, Scott is different from the type of man I usually go for. Completely different.' She swung her legs over the side of the bed, jumped to her feet and linked arms with Elodie. 'Oh, and I haven't even told you the most surprising bit. He's got a five-year-old daughter. And not even that has put me off him. I thought it would. I was sure of it. But nope. I couldn't stop thinking about him all last night. And I'm still thinking about him this morning.'

'The man has a daughter? And you're still interested in him? I'm astonished. This is serious. But if he has a kid, you can't mess this guy around like you have Bentley. Wait. Please tell me he's divorced.'

'Widowed. Or is it widowered? Whatever. His wife died four years ago. And I don't intend to mess him around. I think ... I think he could be The One, El. Why are you looking at me like that?'

'The One? Are you serious?'

'I think so. I don't know. Maybe. You remember how you said you felt when you first saw Archer? Well that's how I felt when I first saw Scott. Okay. That's not strictly true. When I first saw him I thought he was a mugger. But when I realised he wasn't, and he stepped into the moonlight, wow.' She placed a hand on her heart and fluttered her eyelashes. 'I can honestly say I've never felt anything like it. And when we kissed. W-o-w! I thought I'd died and gone to paradise. I was sooooo disappointed when he said he'd better go before the nanny sent out a search party. But I was ... euphoric when he said he'd like to see me again. And I can't remember the last time I felt euphoric.'

'I don't think I've ever heard you say that. If you're really serious about this, then I'm thrilled for you, Iris.'

'That's what I wanted to hear.' Iris smiled as they headed towards the stairs. 'But there might be one small problem. His dead wife's best friend is now the daughter's nanny. I have no idea what she's like, or whether or not she's interested in Scott, but I do know she's here on holiday with him and Ava. That's Scott's daughter. Trisha is the nanny. Only she's not a nanny by profession. I don't know what she is. He didn't say. But if this is going to go anywhere, I need to get her to like me, don't I? Any advice on that?'

Elodie looked completely perplexed. 'I think you need to run that all by me again, because I'm not sure I understood any of it. But there is one thing I am sure of. You're going to have to talk to Bentley. And the sooner you do that, the better. For everyone concerned. I just hope you're right about him not being broken hearted.'

'I'm sure he'll be fine.' Iris hoped he would be. Bentley might not be the perfect guy for her, but Elodie was right, he was lovely. The last thing Iris wanted was to hurt him. 'I'll talk to him after breakfast.'

Chapter 8

Rosie wasn't happy. The last time she had been this upset was when she met Hermione Dunmore at Stanley's funeral, and discovered Hermione was the love of Stanley's life. And now this!

No. This was too much.

She had hoped a good night's sleep would've made this impossible situation better. Except she hadn't slept at all, and if anything, things seemed worse this morning than they had when Will had broken the news to her on Friday night.

Rosie loved a piece of juicy gossip more than most, but this beggared belief. Not that it was gossip. She had heard it from Will's own lips.

He had been waiting for her in the kitchen when she returned from her solo run and he called out to her the moment she opened the front door. She saw him pour two large glasses of chilled white wine as she went to join him; he took a swig of his and topped it up again before handing the other glass to her.

Her intuition told her something wasn't right. First, he had missed their evening run and now he had wine, and by the look of it, supper, waiting.

'What's going on, Will? And why didn't you reply to my text? If you hadn't wanted to run this evening, you could've mentioned it when we left the church.'

'Sorry, Rosie. I didn't see your text until ten minutes ago. There didn't seem much point in responding, because I knew you'd be home before long. And here you are.' He gave her a sheepish smile before taking another large gulp of his wine. 'I'm cooking your favourite pasta dish.'

'Spaghetti alle vongole? That's very kind of you. But I was going to ask if you'd like to join me for supper in the pub.' She was hoping Will would help her get the details of Archer and Elodie's earlier than planned, departure.

'Ah.' He glanced around at the garlic on the chopping board, the clams in the glass bowl, and the saucepans on the hob, and looked decidedly flustered. 'I've started preparing it now. And … we need to have a chat. I … I have some news.'

Rosie took a mouthful of the refreshingly cool wine. A knot was forming in her stomach and Will was making her oddly anxious.

'News? What sort of news?'

'Good news.'

His smile seemed strained and he nervously licked his lips. This was worrying.

'Do I have time for a shower?'

'Of course. Yes. It only takes a few minutes to cook the garlic, clams and wine. I'll put the pasta on to simmer and hold off on the rest until you're back.'

'I'll be quick,' she said.

And she was. But in the few minutes she took to shower – beneath a tepid drizzle, because the damn thing still hadn't been fixed, Will had drained his glass and opened a second bottle. Now she was seriously worried.

'What's the news then?' she asked, as Will topped up her wine glass that she'd left on the kitchen table.

His face was flushed, but not just from the heat of the hob or the amount of wine he was drinking; the man was blushing. Her brother was actually blushing. And his face was growing more crimson by the second.

Either that, or he might be having a heart attack.

'Will? Are you okay?' She reached out and touched his arm. It felt hot and clammy. 'Should I call a doctor?'

'Good heavens, no!' The surprise on his face almost made her laugh with relief. 'It's nothing like that. It's ... simply a trifle ... awkward. No. Not awkward. That's not right at all. It's ... delicate.'

'Delicate? Just spit it out, Will. You know there is nothing that you can't tell me.'

'I ... Let's eat first. Please. I'd prefer that.'

'And I'd prefer not to be kept in suspense. Is it something serious? Is it good news or bad? Oh. You said it was good before I went to shower. Is it about someone we know well? Or is it about you? Oh Good grief! You're not being sent to a new parish, are you? Not after all the years we've been here.'

'No. It's nothing like that. And it's very good news. At least it is for me. And I hope it is for you. Please be patient for a little longer. I shouldn't have said anything until after we'd eaten.'

Rosie had never eaten so fast. She adored Spaghetti alle vongole and would normally savour every bite, but it hardly touched the sides.

'We've eaten,' she said, less than twenty minutes later, pushing her plate to one side. 'Now tell me your news.'

But as soon as she heard it, she sincerely wished she hadn't.

'Say something, Rosie,' Will had said, when her only reactions had been a sort of strangled scream followed by open-mouthed, stunned silence. 'Please. I realise this has come as a complete surprise, and I apologise for keeping it a secret. I couldn't believe it myself, at first. I even tried to deny it. But the truth will out, as they say.' He gave her an apologetic smile and reached out for her hand. 'I thought you might have guessed and you were simply waiting for me to confirm it. I see now that was not the case. I thought ... I hoped you would be happy for me. Nothing will change between us, Rosie, if that is your concern.'

She managed to pull herself together and even contorted her face into what she hoped was a smile.

'I am happy for you, Will. You're my brother and I love you. But ... I had no idea. None at all. How could I have missed the signs? How could I be so blind?'

Will made a small shrug and shook his head slowly as if it was still sinking in with him and he couldn't quite believe it himself.

'I know. After all these years. Life is a mystery. A wonderful journey on a path strewn with miracles.'

What? That made her stare at him intently. He didn't sound like the Will she knew. Perhaps he was having a breakdown. He even looked different somehow. But she soon realised that was merely because he was happy. She couldn't deny him that. Will deserved happiness. He deserved the best that life could offer. She finally put her own feelings to one side and told him so.

But she had been in a foul mood ever since, although she tried to conceal that from her brother. Not even running made her feel better.

Neither did her online gambling. In fact that only made her feel worse. She was in such a bad mood that she wasn't concentrating or carefully placing her bets. By Saturday evening she had lost a considerable sum, and no matter whether she played Poker, Roulette, Blackjack, or the online slots, her losing streak continued. She was a registered player on five separate online casinos, but despite switching between all five, her luck simply wouldn't improve.

She should've stopped after the first few losses, she knew that; those were her normal rules. But Will's news had changed all that.

Nothing was normal now. Everything was different. Her life would never be the same again. And she had no idea how to comes to terms with that.

Will's future might be looking bright; Rosie's definitely wasn't.

Chapter 9

Wet weather was forecast until Monday so Stella wasn't surprised to see drizzle when she opened her curtains at 7.00 on Sunday morning, but by 9.30, when she would normally leave for church, the rain had attained biblical proportions. Only ducks or fools would go out in that, and Stella was neither. Although she had to admit to behaving like a fool since receiving Marian's postcard.

She had repeatedly told herself to act her age; to pull herself together; to stop behaving like a teenager with a crush, but within minutes of each admonishment, her mind wandered back to that fateful time; that incredible year, when she had given both her heart and her body willingly and wantonly to a man she could never have.

Every time she closed her eyes, she could see him. With each breath the fresh citrus scent of the lemon groves; the subtle, dry, woody aroma of the olive trees, and the deep, heady fragrance of lavender pervaded her nostrils. It was as if she were standing once more, on that rich, fertile soil on the hills behind Menton; the hustle and bustle of the French Riviera less than two kilometres away. But it might as well have been a million miles.

Why was this all coming back to her so vividly now? Was it as a result of missing Marian? Was it because she was feeling lonely? Was it because her own mortality was growing ever closer?

She must snap out of this. Self-pity was not a trait Stella admired. Perhaps she should brave the weather and go to church.

The howling wind bending the trees almost in two, and the torrential rain lashing the windows made her think twice. Even the usually tranquil water in the bay of Clementine Cove was distinctly choppy, to say the least.

She glanced towards The Lighthouse rocks, a section of which she could see from her sitting room window, together with the top floor of The Lighthouse tower and the automated light above that. On Friday, Rosie told her that a family of three, one of whom was a small child, had arrived at The Lighthouse and she had commented that she thought it was a strange place to take someone so young. The tide was high this morning and no doubt angry waves whipped up by the weather would be battering The Lighthouse and the rocks below. Would the child be scared, or excited?

Marian was always excited by storms when she was young. She would sit in the windows of Cove Cottage and squeal with delight when a storm hit, constantly interrupting her mother and Stella's conversations to inform them how high the waves had reached on The Lighthouse, most of which was visible from Cove Cottage. That was several years before Marian's parents passed away and many years prior to Marian converting the ground floor of the cottage into a café.

But Marian had been safe on the mainland; being in The Lighthouse itself during such a storm might be an entirely different experience. Stella hoped the little girl and her family weren't scared. In weather like this, they had no option but to remain inside. The sandbank walkway would be under a metre or two of wild water today, and using the rowboat to get ashore would potentially be suicide on such a day.

Should she telephone Cordelia and Charles and ask them to check on the family?

No. Although both Charles and Cordelia were mainly driven by their mutual love of money, Charles did have some common sense. He would've explained all the dos and don'ts in detail, and all the safety procedures and telephone numbers of emergency services were displayed beside the front door of The Lighthouse. Stella had seen that when Cordelia had given her, Rosie and Will a guided tour several years before, not long after the Kings had acquired the property and refurbished it for rental purposes.

Stella had been impressed and so had Will. Rosie had curled her lip and stated that although it was not somewhere she would consider renting, she could see why some other people might. Coming from Rosie, that was a compliment.

The shrill ring of her landline phone made Stella jump. Rosie's number flashed up on the caller display and when Stella answered, it was evident that Rosie wasn't in a good mood.

'You really must get connected to the internet, or at the very least, keep your mobile phone switched on. Why you insist on turning the thing off is beyond me. We'll talk about it on Monday at the reopening of Cove Café. Meet me there at 10 a.m. And don't be late. Archer may be giving out free coffees or cakes to the first few customers. He needs to do something to entice people back. The place has been shut for weeks and we're all getting used to having to go to Millside for coffee and cake. Anyway, the reason I'm calling is to tell you Will's cancelled the morning service. The weather is so atrocious and he doesn't want anyone venturing out unnecessarily. He'll be conducting a service via Zoom. Which you'd be able to join if you had a broadband connection. And I wouldn't have needed to call you. You could have simply read the email I sent out to the parishioners, earlier. I think this storm is worse than the one that brought Parker Sanderson and his yacht to the safety of Clementine Cove, don't you? I don't suppose you've had any updates on Archer and Elodie's departure, have you? I was hoping to go to the pub again myself but ... well, let's just say I've had a nasty shock. Don't tell Will I said "nasty". But it was. I can't tell you about it, because he's sworn me to secrecy. Which is most annoying, because I really need to talk about it to someone other than Will. I'm hoping I'll be able to by tomorrow. So don't be late. 10 a.m. sharp, remember. I must go. Surprisingly, you're not the only one still living in the dark ages. Two others are as behind the times as you. But they're both in their nineties, so that's almost forgivable. Goodbye.'

And with that, Rosie rang off, leaving Stella to assimilate all that Rosie had said.

Chapter 10

Iris wasn't sure what was going on, both with her feelings and with her life in general. She ranged between euphoria and mild depression. Okay, maybe not depression, but she definitely felt sad. And then she felt happy again.

She had met the man of her dreams. Potentially. But he was a widower with a young child. Her best friend, Elodie was leaving the village. But it wouldn't be forever. She hoped. And she could make new friends. Perhaps she already had. Scott was very friendly on Friday night. But she wanted him to be more than a friend. There was a chance he might be The One. On Friday night he had told her he would like to see her again; but she hadn't seen him since. He had at least called her, early on Saturday morning.

'I can't believe it,' he said. 'The words are pouring out of me. I've been up all night.'

'Curry does that to me,' she joked, immediately regretting it. Thankfully he laughed.

'And me. But we had fish fingers, peas and chips for tea, so it couldn't have been that. What can I tell you? My daughter's five and has questionable taste in food. It's you. You're obviously my muse.'

'Wow. I've never been a muse before. I'll add it to my CV. And for the record, there is nothing questionable about fish fingers, peas and chips. It happens to be one of my favourite meals.'

'Excellent. Next time we have them, we'll invite you round.'

'It's a date.'

The tone of his voice changed, becoming more sensual, yet anxious, and substantially less light-hearted.

'Speaking of dates. I meant what I said last night. I really would like to see you again.'

Iris' heart did a little jig.

'I'd like to see you again too.'

'That's great. But having Ava makes things a little more complicated as I'm sure you understand.'

'Er. Is this your way of letting me down nicely?'

'No. Definitely not. I'm simply laying my cards on the table. I haven't dated anyone since Veronica passed away. The only woman Ava has seen me with, is Trisha. Not in a romantic way, obviously. But I don't know how Ava will react when I tell her I'm interested in taking someone on a date.'

'Do you have to tell her?'

'Yes.' He sounded as if he was surprised she asked. 'She's my daughter. I don't keep things from my daughter.'

'I get that. But didn't you say she's five? Does a five-year-old understand dating?'

He gave a snort of laughter. 'They understand a lot more than you might imagine. And Ava's very bright for her age.'

'Couldn't you just say you're meeting a friend for a drink? That wouldn't be a lie. I don't know anything about bringing up a child, but surely it's worse to make a big deal out of something that might turn out to be nothing, isn't it? I mean, I'm not saying this is nothing. It's definitely something. At least I think it is. But ... Okay. I don't know what else to say. I think I'll shut up.' She ended with what was meant to be a jovial laugh but sounded slightly maniacal.

'For someone who says they don't know anything about bringing up a child, your suggestion makes far more sense than mine. You're right. At this stage we are merely two people who like one another, wanting to see if they might like one another even more. No point in making it a big deal just yet. I'll run it by Trisha and see what she thinks.'

'Er. Do you need to get your nanny's permission to date me?' Iris hadn't meant to say that out loud. But come on. Was he for real?

To her relief, he laughed.

'No, Iris. I don't. I meant I'll ask Trisha what she thinks I should tell Ava. She's known Ava since birth, and whether I like to admit it or not, Trisha sometimes knows better than I do, how Ava might react to a certain situation. Not often, but sometimes. And I think this might be one of those situations.'

'O-kay. I'll leave that with you.'

'I'd like to see you right now, but I think I need to get some sleep having been writing all night. And then I want to spend some time with Ava, one-to-one. And I think Trisha might have made plans for tonight. What about tomorrow? Are you free tomorrow evening?'

Iris was disappointed but she made light of it. 'I'll need to check my social calendar. Muses are in such demand, I'll have you know. But I think I can squeeze you in between dusk and dawn. And no, they're not two friends of mine. It'll just be me doing the squeezing.'

He laughed, but when he replied he sounded as though he'd swallowed gravel. 'I like the sound of being squeezed between dusk and dawn, especially if it's just by you. You do know, don't you, how much I wanted to stay last night? But, as I said, it's not that simple.'

'I know. And I hope I made it clear how much I wanted you to stay.'

'You did, Iris. You definitely did. That's why I stayed up all night to write. There was no way I was getting any sleep unless I did something to keep my mind from thinking about you.'

'I didn't get much sleep last night either. I couldn't stop thinking about you.'

There was a momentary silence before either spoke again.

'You probably won't believe this,' Scott said, 'and I normally wouldn't believe such things myself, but I think I was meant to come here. I had a severe case of writer's block. I couldn't get into the heads, or the hearts, of my characters. And don't even get me started on the plot problems I was having. This thriller is set in a cove a bit like this one, and a lighthouse plays a large part in the story. Trisha was doing me a favour and surfing the net for lighthouses in the hope that one might give me some inspiration. She spotted The Lighthouse here, and saw that it was a holiday rental. She called to see if I could come down for the day and have a look around and the owners told her they'd just had a cancellation of a booking for an entire month. Trisha showed it to me right away. And the timing couldn't have been more perfect. Asbestos was discovered in the ceilings of several rooms in Ava's school, so it had to close. While they're sorting out alternative premises, Ava's being homeschooled. I've already told you how Trisha recently lost her job, so was free to fill in as Ava's nanny-come-teacher. So you see. Everything fell into place. Isn't that incredible? If I wrote that happening in one of my books, no one would believe it.'

'Wow. That is really amazing. People say life is stranger than fiction. This proves it actually is.'

He gave a small cough, as if he felt he'd said too much. 'I hope you're not calling me strange.'

Iris laughed. 'A little, maybe. But you're in luck. I love strange men. Oh wait. That didn't come out right.'

'I think it came out perfectly. I'll see you tomorrow, Iris. And at the risk of sounding corny, I'm counting the hours.'

Iris had to tell Bentley that things were over between them. And she had to do it as soon as possible. If she could get the man to stand still for more than two minutes at a time, she would. But Bentley had suddenly become decidedly elusive. And Iris wasn't quite sure why.

Did he already know about her and Scott? Had he seen them together? Maybe kissing on her doorstep? Had Bentley thought Iris might change her mind on Friday night and gone to join her in Clementine Cottage only to be faced with her and Scott in a passionate embrace?

No. He would have said so if he had? Wouldn't he?

He probably would have told Archer.

Iris called Elodie and persuaded her to ask Archer if Bentley had spoken to him about seeing Iris with another man.

'Why is your life so complicated?' Elodie had said. But she asked Archer anyway, and called Iris later.

'No. Bentley hasn't said a word to Archer about seeing you with someone else. He hasn't mentioned you to Archer at all since Friday night. But he did mention bumping into someone from his college days.'

'Really?' Iris was surprised by that. Bentley hadn't said anything to her. But then again, since Iris left the pub on Friday evening, she and Bentley hadn't exchanged more than a few words between them. 'He hasn't mentioned it to me. When was that?

And more importantly, who was it? And where? He hasn't left Clementine Cove in weeks, as far as I know. Oh my God. You don't think it could be Scott, do you? How weird would that be? They say it's a small world. And it would be just my luck that the man I've been sleeping with is a friend of the man I would like to replace him. I know that's not grammatically correct, but we're talking sex here.'

'What?' Elodie laughed. 'I'm glad Archer and I are leaving on Friday. I don't think I can cope with much more of this.'

'Imagine how I feel!' Iris exclaimed, laughing too. 'You're right. Why is my life so complicated?'

'Because you make it complicated. But in answer to your question. Or should I say, questions. Archer didn't say when, or who, or where.' Elodie sighed into the phone. 'I suppose you want me to ask Archer to find out, don't you? I mean, it's not as if we've got anything else to do, other than sort out your love life. We don't have to pack for the trip of a lifetime. Or finish a thousand things before we leave. Or reopen a café. Or launch a brand new restaurant.'

'Okay. I get the point. I'll find out for myself.'

'Great. But when you do, don't forget to tell me. Because now you've got me wondering who this mystery person might be.'

Iris eventually tracked Bentley down. He was making some last-minute alterations to the display in the window of the refurbished Cove Café. Marian had always had a variety of cakes; some real, some imitation because the sun would turn real cakes in the front of the window, to mush, but Bentley was going for a different look. Iris wasn't quite sure what it was but didn't say that to Bentley.

'Looking good,' she said, poking her head round the door. 'The display, I mean, not you. Oh. Not that you're not looking good too. Although you've got a large blue smear of something on your cheek. You might want to get that.'

He seemed surprised to see her but he smiled, wiped his cheek with his sleeve and backed out of the window, although he didn't move towards her.

'Is it gone?'

Iris nodded. 'Yep. All gone. Er. I've been trying to have a chat with you all day. We seem to be missing each other's texts and calls.'

'I know,' he said. 'We need to talk. Would you like a drink?'

'Do you have any wine? I know the Bistro isn't open until Thursday but I thought...' she let her voice trail off as Bentley disappeared into the kitchen. 'I'll talk to myself then, shall I?' she mumbled.

He returned seconds later with a bottle of white wine and two glasses.

'We've stocked the wine chiller to ensure it works properly. Unlike the fridge that arrived this morning. The thing blew a fuse the second I plugged it in. And it cost a bloody fortune. They're replacing it free of charge, obviously, but I don't want another incident so close to opening.'

'That's a pain.'

'That's one word for it.'

She watched him pour the wine and he handed her a glass. Right now, the whole place felt somewhat icy. She could cut the tension with a knife.

'I hear you bumped into an old friend,' Iris said, after taking a sip of her wine.

She wasn't sure how she had expected him to react, but spitting a mouthful of wine over the table wasn't on her list.

He wiped drips from his chin, once again using his sleeve. Didn't the man have a napkin, or a paper serviette? It was a café, after all.

'Who told you that? Elodie, I suppose. Archer obviously told her.'

'Was it meant to be a secret? What's the big deal? Was it a long-lost lover or something?'

'Yes,' he said. 'And no. It wasn't a secret. But I ... I wasn't sure how to tell you. That's why I've been avoiding you all day.'

Now it was Iris who spat out her wine, but she managed to put her hand in front of her mouth, and she yanked a tissue from her handbag to wipe up the liquid.

'What? You ... you've been avoiding me? On purpose? Why?'

He shook his head and took another gulp of wine. This time he swallowed it before continuing.

'Because I didn't know how I felt about it, and I didn't want to say anything until I did. The last thing I want is to hurt you, Iris. You're fantastic and I really like you. The sex is great. We both know that. But ...'

It took her a while to comprehend what he was saying but when he stopped for a breath, she jumped in.

'Hey! Hold on Mister! That's my speech.'

'Your speech? I don't understand.'

They stared at one another for a second or two.

'Are you dumping me?' Iris asked, unsure if she was relieved or insulted.

'Were you intending to dump me?' he countered.

'Yes,' she said, smiling a little. 'Although technically, we weren't dating as such. Just friends who had sex.'

'Ah. The old 'friends with benefits' scenario.'

'That's what it was, Bentley. Did you think I wanted it to be more?'

He shook his head. 'I didn't think so. But I wasn't sure. We never discussed how we felt about each other. I was nuts about you, at the start.'

'I know. I felt the same, I think. I always knew we wouldn't last though.'

'Me too. But it was fun while it did. And I meant what I said about the sex. It really was fantastic.'

'Yeah. Do you think we'll miss it?'

'Only if we're not having great sex with someone else.'

She eyed him over the rim of her glass. 'I take it from that comment that there's someone you're hoping to have sex with in the not-too-distant future.' She sat forward on her chair. 'Wait! It's not the long-lost lover you bumped into, is it? She's here? In Clementine Cove? I'm assuming it's a she, but whatever.'

He grinned at her. 'Yes. On both counts. I couldn't believe it when I saw her. Nor could she. We haven't seen one another since we did our first culinary science course and ended up working part time in the same restaurant as a waiter and waitress, to help pay our bills to get us through uni. We hit it off from the word go and within weeks we'd moved into a grotty bedsit together. It was truly a shithole but we thought it was paradise. Our little love-nest. Until she was offered a position she couldn't turn down, from a family friend. In Manchester, for God's sake. I'd already accepted a position at a top London restaurant. Neither of us wanted to give up on our dreams of becoming great chefs. We tried to make the distance thing work but restaurant hours and long-distance relationships are not compatible. We drifted apart and eventually lost touch. And then I saw her yesterday, here in Clementine Cove, getting into a boat, and it felt like time had been turned back. We chatted. And she told me how she had come to be here. It was as if it was meant to be. And then she had to go. She's looking after her friend's child and ... Iris? What's wrong? Why are you laughing hysterically?'

Iris tried to control herself, but this was too much. 'Her name is Trisha, isn't it?' she managed.

Bentley furrowed his brows. 'How did you know that?'

'Give me a m-minute.' For some reason, she simply couldn't stop laughing.

And later, when Iris and Bentley told Elodie and Archer, over a glass of wine in The

Bow and Quiver, they couldn't believe it either.

'Small world?' Iris said, as all four of them discussed the odds of something like this happening. 'The bloody planet is minuscule.'

Chapter 11

Things didn't seem quite so amusing on Sunday.

Trisha, Scott and Ava were stuck inside The Lighthouse, for their own safety as well as their comfort, due to the appalling weather, which meant that Iris would not be seeing Scott that evening. Iris knew that, long before he called to confirm it.

But what she didn't expect was his response when she mentioned Trisha and Bentley.

She was aware of Trisha's reaction when Bentley had told her that he and Iris had been hooking up from time to time since Christmas, but were really just good friends. Friends who would no longer be having sex with one another – which is what he and Iris had agreed they'd say.

Trisha didn't seem to find that news quite as amazing as Iris and Bentley had hoped.

'She didn't seem very pleased,' he said to Iris on the phone, early on Sunday morning.

'What did she say, exactly?' Iris queried. She was debating whether or not to call Scott and tell him about the situation herself, and she needed to know how Trisha had taken it.

'She was surprised. She was also a little upset that I hadn't mentioned it earlier. And then she asked me how she could be sure that you and I wouldn't be hooking up again.'

'Oh crikey. That's not good. Do you know if she's told Scott?'

'No idea,' Bentley said. 'But I think it's safe to assume she will if she hasn't done so already, don't you?'

'Yes. But that's why I didn't want to phone Scott last night and tell him about it. Doing that would make it seem more important than it is. No offence, Bentley.'

'None taken. I get it. Perhaps I shouldn't have told Trisha.'

'Maybe not. But you know this village better than I do. It was bound to come out. Someone would have mentioned it. And then it would've looked worse than it really is.'

'I don't see what the fuss is about,' Bentley said. 'People break up with one another every day of the week. We weren't even dating, in reality. And neither of us has been hurt. So what's the issue? I told Trisha we won't be having sex again. Why can't she just believe that?'

'Men lie,' Iris said. 'Actually, women lie too, so don't take that personally.'

'I won't. But I don't lie. Why is she assuming I might? I didn't lie to her all those years ago. What makes her think I'll do so now?'

'I think you need to have this conversation with Trisha.'

'I would. But I can't. After I told her about us at the end of our date last night, she said she needed time to think. I walked her back to The Lighthouse, over the sandbank path, and she hardly said a word. I was rambling on about how there was nothing between you and me and that even though the sex was great and that you're a fantastic person, we both knew we didn't have a future together. She asked me if sex with you was better than it had been with her, and when I told her I couldn't really remember what sex was like with her, because it was so long ago, she told me I wasn't going to get a chance to compare it now.'

'Oh dear God, Bentley. Why didn't you just say sex with her was much, much better?'

'Because I honestly couldn't remember if it was or not. And I don't tell lies.'

'Okay. That's fair enough. That's actually a point in your favour. But you need to tell her that. Why can't you?'

'She's turned off her phone. I called and left her several messages and now it's off completely. I can't get across the sandbank and I'm not getting in a boat, even for her. I'll have to wait until the weather clears and try to explain it then.'

'Okay. I don't think I should call Scott. I'll wait until he calls me. And then I'll play the whole thing down and I'll try to make him see how silly Trisha is being. Because she is being silly, Bentley. Your relationship with her was years ago. She must realise you've slept with more than just me since then.'

'She knows that. But for some reason, she seems to be fixated on you.'

'Fixated on me? Why? We haven't even met. Oh wait. Maybe Scott has told her about me. He was going to ask her advice about telling his kid that he's taking me out on a date. I thought it was a good thing. Maybe it's not. Especially now. She adores Ava, Scott's child. And she was his wife's best friend. She's going to be protective of them both, isn't she? Perhaps she now sees me as some sort of...'

'Tart?'

'Not the word I was looking for, but thanks.'

'Harlot?'

'Bentley. Stop now. I was thinking along the lines of some sort of free spirit. The type of woman who doesn't take relationships seriously. Who doesn't get involved emotionally. That's probably not the type of woman she wants to see Scott dating. I think I may have some explaining to do. But Scott's got a good sense of humour. And I've got one thing in my favour. I told him the night we met that I was seeing someone purely for sex. And he didn't seem to mind at all.'

But when Scott called Iris later that morning and she mentioned Trisha and Bentley and how incredible it was that they knew one another, he clearly wasn't thrilled.

'Trisha's upset,' he said.

'Why? Bentley is so excited to have seen her again. He can't stop talking about her. It's Trisha this and Trisha that. I'd say he's at risk of being as much in love with her now as he apparently was all those years ago.'

'And doesn't that bother you at all?'

'No. Why should it? I'm happy for him. I told you on Friday night that he and I just had sex and there was nothing else between us. Other than the fact we're friends. I didn't tell you his name because it didn't really matter. And it was funny because I was trying to find him on Saturday morning to tell him that we wouldn't be having sex again and he was trying to find me to tell me the same thing. Because I'd met you, and he'd met Trisha. Again.'

'Why is that funny?'

'Okay. Maybe funny isn't the right word. The point is, Bentley and I were just friends who had sex. Now we're still friends, but friends who don't have sex and won't be having sex again. Not with one another. But hopefully with other people. Are you upset about this? Because if you are, I don't get it. Nothing's changed since Friday night.'

'Sadly, it has. I hoped that you and Trisha would get on. Would become friends, if you and I ... if this went anywhere. Now that's highly unlikely. And that's a massive problem. Ava adores Trisha, and Trisha adores Ava. Trisha is the closest thing to a mum that Ava's ever had. She was too young to remember Veronica, as I explained. If I ever ... want to be with someone else, it has to be someone that Trisha likes, respects, and can be good friends with. I've known for years about the man Trisha lived with all that time ago. She told Veronica that letting him go was her one big regret. Surely you can see that is a bit of a stumbling block?'

'Er ... no. I can't. Yes of course I get the bit about her and Ava. And of course it's important that Trisha likes the woman, or women you date, and that if you choose to spend the rest of your life with someone, that person needs to get on well with Trisha. But come on, Scott. We're all grown-ups here. Apart from Ava. And we can get on with anyone, if we choose to. I'm not a bad person. I've got a few faults, I'll readily admit to that, but no one's perfect. And I was upfront about Bentley. I didn't try to hide it or sugar coat it. It was what it was. It's now completely over. But the fact we're still friends must score in our favour, surely? Bentley is a lovely guy. Anyone will tell you that. I think Trisha needs to give the man a chance. I mean for heaven's sake. They haven't seen one another in God knows how many years. Did she expect him to take a vow of celibacy or something? And even after all those years, the guy's still crazy about her. That must count for a lot. Plus, if Bentley was so important to Trisha and letting him go was her one big regret, why hasn't she tried to find him? It's easy to find anyone on the internet these days. And Bentley doesn't exactly hide himself under a bushel. He's on every social media platform on the planet. Especially now that he and Archer are opening a new Café Bistro.'

'Have you finished?' His tone was friendly, even if his words weren't.

'I'm not sure. Are you less, or more, inclined to see me, now that I've said all that?'

She couldn't recall exactly what she had said. For some reason this bloody Trisha woman was making Iris see red.

'I'm not sure either. But I do like your passion. And your loyalty. And I like the fact you haven't said anything bad about Trisha, other than that she needs to face reality, and that she's too lazy to get off her bum and find the man she tells everyone she's loved for most of her life.' He laughed then. 'Veronica would've said something similar if she'd been here today.'

'If she'd been here today, we wouldn't be having this conversation. Oh God. Now I've gone too far, haven't I? I did say I have faults. One of them is not knowing when to keep my mouth shut. Can you forget I said that?'

After a momentary silence he said, 'More inclined to see you again, I think. And I don't need to forget it. Veronica would've liked you. Even if Trisha doesn't.'

'Woohoo! Wait. What? Trisha doesn't like me? She hasn't even met me. That's a bit unfair.'

'Iris?'

'Yes.'

'It's time to keep your mouth shut.'

His laughter made it difficult to tell if he was serious about that or not.

Iris erred on the side of caution.

'Consider it shut. But hold on a minute. Can you ask Trisha to turn her phone back on, please, and to talk to Bentley? He really is a lovely guy. And everyone deserves a second chance. Especially on a stormy Sunday. I swear to you, if the man could get to that lighthouse without killing himself in the process, he would.'

'I'll try my best. And I'll also ask her to give you a second chance too. I'll call you in the morning. Assuming this lighthouse doesn't get swept away.'

'It won't. It's been through worse storms than this. But how is Ava coping? Sorry. I should've asked sooner.'

'Ava is loving every second of it. I'm the one having a panic attack.'

Iris could tell he was joking. At least about himself. And she couldn't wait to see him again. As for Trisha, Iris could definitely wait to meet her. In fact the longer she could put that off, the better.

Chapter 12

Monday dawned with lemon-coloured splotches mingled with pink candyfloss puffs of cloud, chased away by a golden sunrise in an impossibly blue sky, causing those who were awake early enough to see it, to comment on the strange weather patterns recently. One day brought black clouds, high winds and torrential rain; the next brought rainbow clouds fit for a fairy tale and the promise of a day filled with sunshine and warm breezes.

Iris was awake, and she was as bright and breezy as the weather. Although it had taken two large mugs of coffee and a three-tiered bacon, egg and mushroom toastie to make her feel that way. And the knowledge that she might see Scott today.

He had called her again last night, to tell her he'd had a chat with Trisha and things were looking good. At least on the Bentley front.

'I reminded her that we can lose those we love when we least expect it, and that life is too short to throw away any chances we may have to find happiness,' he said. 'I reminded myself of that too.'

That sounded hopeful, both for Bentley and for herself.

She considered calling Bentley to tell him the good news, a second after she said goodbye to Scott, but she decided she should wait. Trisha might try to call him and the last thing Iris wanted was for Bentley's phone to be engaged.

Later she received a text from him with a smiley face, a heart and the words, 'We'll talk tomorrow. Need to get some sleep.'

The poor man was rushed off his feet what with everything going on with the café and the restaurant and Iris was determined to do something to help. She had no clients booked for the next few days. Her business as a voice coach had suffered since she'd moved to Clementine Cove. Not that it bothered her. She made enough to be happy, and her cottage was rent-free, her dad having inherited it from his brother, Stanley Talbot, deceased. If and when she needed extra cash, she could call up any one of several businesses, film studios, theatres, and more, in London, and clients would pay her virtually any fee she asked for, such was her reputation for being able to achieve the almost unachievable, and to train anyone's voice to do extraordinary things.

Cove Café was reopening at 10.00 a.m. and the new waitress, Harley would have her hands full. Iris had heard several of the locals say they would be there on the dot, and while there would not be a stampede, it might still prove to be slightly intimidating for Harley.

Rosie Parker, for one, would no doubt try to make Harley's job difficult. Harley lived on the new estate, which made her a member of The Great Unwashed, as Rosie liked to call the residents. Rosie was not a fan. Hopefully though, as Rosie was the vicar's sister, she would refrain from being blatantly rude.

Or maybe not. One could never be sure how Rosie might behave. Marian had told Iris and Elodie several tales of snide remarks Rosie had made, of people the woman had upset, of things in the village she had tried to stop from happening.

Rosie Parker, or Nosy Parker as she was known by those brave enough to say it, was not a good role model for Christianity, but she did unwittingly provide some amusement amongst the locals.

Iris missed Marian sometimes, and today Marian would be missed by everyone who knew her. But Archer had a plan, which Elodie shared with Iris. A TV screen had been installed on one wall of the Cove Café Bistro and unbeknown to all, including Stella herself, Marian would appear via a video link and she would ask Stella Pinkheart to cut the ribbon of the refurbished Cove Café.

It was a kind and thoughtful gesture, and Iris was pleased that Archer had thought of it. Apparently, Marian was thrilled when he'd suggested it to her, but that was just the type of man Archer Rhodes was. Kind, thoughtful and generous. He was also extremely handsome, and according to Elodie, bloody good in bed. Elodie had been lucky to find him. Iris was now hoping she had found something similar herself in Scott Fitzgerald.

It took Iris longer than usual to get ready. She had told Scott about the reopening of the café and he said that he might bring Ava.

'Apart from the fact that I drink copious amounts of coffee, as many writers do, cafés are great places to listen in on other people's conversations,' he said. 'Strictly for research purposes, you understand. And Ava loves balloons, like most girls of her age. You did say there will be balloons didn't you?'

'Absolutely,' Iris confirmed. 'And who doesn't love a balloon?'

She hoped he would be there, and it would give her a chance to meet his daughter. But she wouldn't be disappointed if Trisha stayed away, although Bentley might be.

'You're early,' Archer said, both surprise and amusement in his voice when Iris knocked on the door of Cove Café and he opened it. 'We don't open until 10.00, unless you're here to help?'

'I am. Didn't El tell you I'd offered? But are you saying that you wouldn't let me in if I weren't?' Iris laughed at such an idea. She knew Archer wouldn't turn her away even if all she did was sit in a chair and watch everyone else work.

He stood aside to let her in. 'Nah. You know you're always welcome. But you may regret your offer. There's a list of things to do as long as your arm. I thought we were ready last night. It seems I was wrong.'

'You're here!' Elodie was obviously pleased to see her. 'How can a place get so dusty in one night? It was spotless when we left here yesterday.'

'It's a mystery,' Iris joked. 'But a boring one. What do you need me to do?'

'There's a list over there beside the coffee machine. Take your pick.'

Elodie nodded towards the new, partly screened off, granite counter that ran across the back wall, ending at the kitchen door. The counter housed various machines and other equipment needed to run a thriving café and restaurant business, but only the state-of-the-art coffee machine was visible to customers. Iris hadn't seen it until now. It had been tested and then covered as soon as it arrived, to ensure it didn't get damaged in any way before the big day. It looked like something you'd expect to see on a spaceship.

Iris gasped loudly when she looked at the list. 'I didn't think Archer was serious. He's right. I am regretting my offer.' She laughed and then ran her hand along the gleaming top of the coffee machine. 'But this is impressive. It must've cost a fortune. May I at least have a coffee before I start?'

'Yes,' Bentley replied, appearing from the kitchen with a cardboard box that he gently deposited on a space to one side of the machine. 'It did, and you may. But please let me make it. We'd like to keep this looking pristine at least until the customers arrive.'

'Hey. I won't make a mess. And a good morning to you too, Bentley.' Iris playfully slapped his arm.

Bentley raised his brows. 'I've seen your kitchen counter after you make coffee,' he said, and then he smiled and kissed her on the cheek. 'Good morning, Iris.'

She grinned. 'You'd better not let Trisha see you do that. She'll think we're about to leap into bed or something. And speaking of Trisha, what's the latest?'

'It's looking good. She's going to come to the reopening.' He beamed at Iris before looking over her head. 'Anyone else want a coffee while I'm here?'

'Yes, please,' Elodie and Archer said in unison.

He removed four brand new mugs from the cardboard box, each bearing the equally new logo of Cove Café Bistro on the front. It was an image of Cove Cottage in all its Ruby-red glory, but in the shape of a coffee cup with the thatched roof looking like the froth on top of the coffee, and steam coming out of the chimney, which was made to look like a chocolate flake bar. He rinsed them under the tap in the sink built into the counter, handing each one to Iris to dry.

'These are really snazzy,' she said, wiping them carefully with one of the new tea towels, also bearing the café logo.

Everything in the place matched or complemented the colours of the logo. The bench seats, chairs and tables all had pale Ash wood bases and legs, with gleaming, pearly white tops and backrests, but all the seating had Ruby-red, removable cushions for added comfort for the restaurant clientele. White linen tablecloths emblazoned with the logo would also be added to the tables in the evenings. A clean, fresh and welcoming look for the daytime and a cosy, comfortable look for the evenings.

Bentley placed all four mugs on the base plate of the machine once Iris had dried them.

'This gorgeous beast makes up to four hundred coffees an hour, of various varieties, with just the press of a button,' he informed her. 'All four extraction heads can be used simultaneously. It's got two separate refrigerated containers for different types of milk, and several mugs and heatproof glasses can be stored on the top.'

'Fascinating,' Iris said, meeting Elodie's eye and shaking her head as Bentley placed all four delicious-looking coffees on a tray to the other side of the machine.

'Don't go into the kitchen with him,' Elodie joked. 'He spent twenty minutes telling me about the fridge.'

Bentley gasped and pretended to look hurt. 'It's not a mere fridge,' he said. 'You're all heathens, that's your problem.'

'I feel sorry for Harley already,' Iris said. 'Is she here?'

'No.' Bentley shook his head. 'It's going to be a long day and she'll be the one doing most of the work. We told her to come in around 9.00 which will give her plenty of time to settle in. She's spent quite a bit of time here already, getting to know how everything works and where everything is. She's going to be great. So what do you think of the coffee?'

Iris was taking her first sip as he spoke.

'Give me a chance to taste it.'

She savoured it slowly, closing her eyes and then licking her lips, before making several sounds as if in the throes of having an orgasm, tossing her hair from side to side as she did so.

'Fine,' Bentley said, sounding miffed. 'I've got better things to do than watch you make fun of me.'

Iris laughed. 'Sorry. It's fantastic. Seriously. Definitely the best coffee I've had since Marian left.'

'Praise indeed,' said Archer. 'Marian's coffee was to die for.'

Elodie laughed. 'It's good to know that machine isn't just beautiful to look at, but that it actually makes great coffee too.'

'Right,' said Bentley, looking at Iris. 'You can rinse the rest of the mugs and then stack them on the top of the machine. There's a box with the glasses, in the kitchen.'

'Is that on the list?' Iris asked, grinning.

He grabbed the tea towel she had used and flicked her with it, before folding it in half and placing it on the counter.

'Yes. It's number fifteen. Tick it off when you're done. I'll be in the kitchen if you need me.'

Chapter 13

Stella arrived at Cove Café Bistro at 9.55 precisely. Rosie wasn't the only one who had asked her not to be late for the reopening; Archer phoned her on Sunday evening and said he would like her to be at the front of the queue, so would she mind getting to the café five minutes early.

'I don't expect there to be a horde of eager customers,' he said, 'but I'm sure most of the locals will make an effort to support us, and I know Marian would like you to be at the forefront.'

Tears welled up in Stella's eyes when he said that and she felt like a sentimental fool. Now, as she stood outside of the newly refurbished venue, more tears bubbled up. She knew she would be emotional today but she blinked them back, straightened her shoulders and her back, and held her head high.

A crowd was already gathering and they cheered loudly as Archer and Bentley appeared from the side of the building, the front door being blocked by a large Ruby-red ribbon criss-crossing from top to bottom and side to side. Several matching balloons were tied to the ribbon and they fluttered and bobbed about in the light breeze.

Archer waved at Stella and smiled, beckoning her forward with his hand as he and Bentley approached the front door.

Stella glanced around, in part to look for Rosie, and in part to check that it was her Archer was motioning to and not Elodie, who stood beside her having warmly greeted her a moment earlier.

'He wants you to join them,' Elodie confirmed, a huge smile on her face.

'Me? Oh my goodness. Why?'

'You'll see,' Iris said, appearing by Elodie's side just as a breathless Rosie tapped Stella on the arm, making her jump.

'What's going on?' Rosie asked, all eyes now on Stella as the cheering and clapping grew louder.

'You nearly gave me a heart attack,' Stella said. 'And I have no idea.'

'Come and join us, Stella,' Archer called out above the cacophony of voices.

'Why does Archer want you?' Rosie asked, as Stella moved forward.

'It's a surprise,' Stella heard Elodie say.

Archer reached out and took Stella by the hand, indicating that she should stand between him and Bentley and face the crowd, which she could see was much larger than she had realised.

She wasn't sure what was happening but she was pleased she had made an extra effort to look nice today. She had done so as a sign of respect for Marian, even though she was well aware that Marian wouldn't be there to see it. She wore a Ruby-red dress and matching coat, the colours of Cove Cottage only slightly paler, with black court shoes and a black patent handbag. Her hat was black with a Ruby-red flower and a black feather. She thought she looked very regal and standing here before this crowd made her feel like the Queen.

Bentley held up his hand to silence the throng, and Archer finally spoke.

'Thank you all for coming to help us celebrate the reopening of this beloved café. The name has changed slightly and the interior has a new look but at its heart this is still Marian's café. You'll soon see that, although there are some additions to the menu, Marian's Mega Breakfast and some of her other specials are still here. We hope some, if not all of you will also join us on Thursday evening, for the opening of the new restaurant, but we'll tell you more about that later. We're here to open the café, so let's do that right now.'

Music rang out from inside the building and the front door slowly opened to reveal a pretty young woman wearing a Ruby-red dress beneath a white apron with a Ruby-red logo of Cove Café Bistro emblazoned on the front. She smiled warmly before standing to one side and indicating a TV screen on the wall behind her.

Stella gasped as a beaming, suntanned, Marian popped up on the screen and although the crowd outside would have to peer around Stella to get a good view of Marian, Stella could see her clearly between the criss-crossed ribbon and the balloons.

'Hello, Stella,' Marian said, blowing her a kiss. 'Hello everybody!' She waved joyfully at the crowd.

Everyone whistled and shrieked with delight and yelled back in unison, 'Hello, Marian.'

Some shouted, 'We miss you.'

Others yelled, 'You're looking good.'

Stella burst into tears. But they were tears of joy and she didn't bother to wipe them away.

'Oh, Marian, my angel. It's so wonderful to see you. Are you really here? I mean, I know you're not here in the village, but are you able to see us, right now, or is this a recording?'

She glanced at Archer who took her hand in his and squeezed it.

'She can see us and hear us as clearly as we can see and hear her. But there may be a slight time delay of a second or two.'

'I'm here, Stella,' Marian confirmed, still beaming at her. 'Live and well in the middle of the Med. I'm so thrilled I can be with you today. I'd like to ask you to do the honours and cut the ribbon to declare the café officially reopen. Would you do that for me, Stella? It would mean the world to me if you would. And I know Mum and Dad will be looking down on you and on me and smiling.'

'Me? Cut the ribbon! Oh my darling. I'd be delighted.'

She could hardly see through her tears now but she shot a look at Archer, who nodded as if to confirm this was what he and Bentley also wanted. And then Bentley handed her a pair of scissors.

'Feel free to say a few words if you'd like to,' Archer said, leaning towards her. 'But no problem if you'd rather not.'

Stella took a deep, calming breath and smiled again at Marian and then Archer and Bentley and finally, the crowd.

'Good gracious,' she said. 'This is such a lovely surprise. And such an honour. I apologise for my tears but they're tears of pure happiness. This day is special for all of us, but especially for my darling Marian, and dear Archer and Bentley, who have worked so hard to ensure Cove Café Bistro opened as soon as possible.' She waited until the cheers subsided a little before continuing. 'We've all been missing coming here for the scrumptious cakes and delicious drinks, and we've all been missing Marian. Me more than most, I know. But with the cutting of this ribbon, we'll not only be getting this wonderful café and a superb restaurant, we'll also be able to feel that Marian is with us, at least in her heart and her thoughts, if not in person. Her parents would be so proud if they were here. And without further ado, I declare Cove Café Bistro open. May it flourish and prosper and bring friendship, joy and contentment to all those who cross this threshold.'

She cut the ribbon and it fluttered to the floor releasing the balloons all bearing the new logo, each one slowly drifting skywards as the crowd roared and clapped and cheered. But all Stella could see was Marian and they smiled at one another as if there was no one else around.

'Thank you, Stella,' Marian said. 'Archer's got a little gift from me to you.'

And then, to Stella's astonishment, Archer tapped her on the arm and held an open laptop in front of her. She darted her eyes from it to the big screen and back again. How could Marian be on both screens at the same time?

'I'll show you how it works later, once everyone's settled down,' he said. 'And then you and Marian can chat again later. But for now, take a seat inside, anywhere you like. I'll give you time to say goodbye while I tell this lot what's on offer.'

He winked at her and handed the laptop to the pretty young woman who had opened the door.

'Hi. I'm Harley,' the young woman said. 'Please come in and make yourself at home.'

Stella went inside and glanced around her, gasping at the changes and taking a seat at a table in the window. Harley placed the laptop on the table and turned the screen to face Stella.

'What can I get you?' Harley asked.

'She'll have a Marian's Mega Breakfast and a cappuccino,' Marian said, laughing. 'And this is on us, Stella, so don't even think of getting out your purse. Now it's going to get very loud and very busy in there in a moment or two because Archer and Bentley are telling everyone that the all breakfasts and drinks are free this morning, so I'll say goodbye for now. But as Archer said, we'll chat later, okay? And then you can tell me what you've been doing since I left.'

'That won't take long,' Stella said. 'But I'd rather hear about your adventures. You look so happy, Marian. And thank you for your postcard, by the way.'

'It'll be so good to be able to chat with you,' said Marian. 'And Parker wants to say hello, so he'll be here later, too. Bye then. Have fun today.' Marian waved and blew her another kiss.

'Bye, bye, my darling girl.' Stella blew her several kisses before the screen went blank and then a screensaver popped up.

Harley smiled at Stella. 'It's lovely to meet you. Shall I just close this for now and turn it off?'

'It's lovely to meet you too, Harley. And yes please. If you would. I'm afraid I have no idea how this new-fangled gadgetry works. But after today, I'm determined to find out.'

Chapter 14

Rosie wiped away a tear, surprised that what she'd just witnessed had made her so emotional. She usually wasn't one to get all gooey and tearful over such sentimental claptrap, but she could understand why Stella was, on this occasion. Although behaving like a blubbering idiot did no one any favours.

Looking around her in the crowd she was astonished to see so many people dabbing tissues at their eyes, or blowing their noses, or oohing and ahhing at such utter nonsense.

It was a relief when Archer announced free breakfasts and drinks for all, this morning. Though quite how he planned to accommodate so many people was a mystery, and he could tell everyone else to form an orderly queue but if he expected Rosie to be a part of it he could think again. Stella had been ushered inside. Rosie would join her at her table.

She tutted as she spotted Will. What was he doing here? He had asked her if she was attending the reopening of the café and she had made it clear that she was meeting Stella.

'I might see you there then,' he said, all hopeful smiles.

She had been tempted to reply, 'Not if it's at all possible for me to avoid you.' But she hadn't.

She pushed her way towards Archer.

'I'd arranged to meet Stella here at 10.00 and it's already 10.20 and she's inside. I assume I'm not expected to be pushed and shoved out here, and I can go in and join her.'

'Strictly speaking, you should join the queue like everyone else, Rosie. Just as your brother has. There are no favourites here. Apart from Stella. But on this occasion we'll make an exception.'

'Thank you so much,' she replied, as sarcastically as she could.

Who did the man think he was? No favourites indeed. So Elodie and Iris were expected to queue were they? Like hell they were. They were making their way in right before her eyes, and not only the two of them. A man, a woman and a child were being ushered in by Bentley.

If it weren't for the fact she had arranged to meet Stella, she would walk away and never come back. It was only a café, for heaven's sake.

Wasn't that the child she had seen at The Lighthouse? Those golden curls looked familiar, as did the man and woman. So they were friends of Bentley's were they? She would have to find out more about them. But that would have to wait. She had far more important – and disturbing – matters on her mind.

'There you are!' Rosie flopped onto the seat opposite Stella. 'I'm glad you were sensible enough to get a table in the window. Have you seen the crowd? Where's the waitress? Have you ordered? I hope they've employed more staff for today. At this rate they'll still be queueing at lunchtime.'

'Good morning, Rosie,' Stella said, smiling oddly. 'How are you on this wonderful Monday morning?'

Rosie furrowed her brows. 'How am I? Exhausted. And not only that I'm … I'm … oh! I'm so upset I can't even think of a word to describe how I am.' She leant forward and crossed her arms on the table. 'I've got something to tell you and I know you'll be as stunned and as horrified as I was when he told me. But I've been sworn to secrecy, so you must promise me you'll keep it between us. Although as he's here today, the cat's out of the bag, so that horse has bolted. And you see! I'm so upset I'm getting my idioms mixed.'

'You're doing more than that,' Stella said, the odd smile still firmly in place.

'What is wrong with you today?' Rosie asked.

'Nothing. Absolutely nothing. I couldn't be happier if I tried.'

'Then why are you still blubbering?'

'Because I'm happy. And I can't seem to stop. The dam has burst, I'm afraid.'

'Honestly, Stella. You really need to pull yourself together.'

'Did you see what happened? Did you hear my little speech? You were late, weren't you?'

Rosie tutted. 'Yes I was. My damn shower still isn't fixed. Will assured me he's spoken to the plumbers the diocese recommended, but I don't believe it for a minute. Clearly, he has his mind on other things and probably hasn't called at all. I should do it myself but where does one find a good plumber these days?'

'Excuse me. I'm Harley and I was coming to take your order but I couldn't help hearing what you said about finding a good plumber.'

Rosie glared at the young woman and looked her up and down. 'It's rude to eavesdrop. Didn't anyone teach you that?' Seeing the apron and the logo it was obvious that this must be the new waitress.

'Rosamunde! That's both rude and unnecessary. Harley was, I'm sure, trying to help.' Stella glowered at Rosie, the smile having completely disappeared from Stella's mouth.

'I'm so sorry,' Harley said. 'But I was only trying to help. My dad's a plumber. If you want, I can give him a call and he'll pop round. Or I can give you his number and you can call him if you prefer.'

'You see!' said Stella. 'Now apologise.'

Rosie tutted. 'I'm sorry ... Harley. Your father is a plumber? Is he local? Could he come today?'

Harley smiled and the relief on her face made Rosie feel a pang of guilt. But only a pang.

'Yes. We live in Baker's Lane. I know he's busy but if I ask him, he'll definitely manage to fit you in. Although it might not be until later, if that's okay.'

Baker's Lane was on the new estate. Rosie had forgotten that this girl was one of The Great Unwashed.

'Beggars can't be choosers, I suppose,' Rosie said. 'Please call and ask him. Anytime today will be fine. I'll give you my number and he can text me and let me know when he'll be arriving.'

'I'll call him the second I get a break. What would you like to order?'

'Have you ordered?' Rosie asked Stella, who nodded. 'In that case, I'll have whatever Stella's having. And a large cappuccino. You will call your father won't you? You won't forget.'

Harley smiled. 'I won't forget. I've got a very good memory.'

'And she won't forget how rude you were,' said Stella, when Harley had moved away to take more orders. 'I hope she doesn't spit in your coffee.'

'I told you, I'm upset! Wait. Spit in my coffee! She wouldn't dare. Would she?'

Stella gave Rosie a smile and shrugged before glancing out the window at the crowd.

'There's Will,' she said, pointing to him. 'Why didn't he come in with you?'

'I'm trying to avoid him.'

Stella furrowed her brows. 'Avoid your own brother? Why?'

'I told you why. Because I'm upset.'

'Will's upset you?' Stella looked doubtful. 'How? Oh. Isn't that Penny Walsh beside him? She's lovely, isn't she? I'm rather ashamed I haven't spent more time getting to know her. But she likes to keep herself to herself, doesn't she and—'

'I wish she did!' Rosie snapped. 'Will's spent plenty of time getting to know her. Far too much time. Behind my back, what's more. How could he? If he thinks he can just move her in, he's got another think coming. The diocese will have something to say about it. You mark my words. The woman's a pagan. Literally! What is the man thinking? But will he listen to me? No. I suppose it's some sort of mid-life crisis. I sincerely hope so. He says it's not but he would say that, wouldn't he? There, you see! You've guessed what's happening without me having to tell you.'

'Guessed what's...?' Stella darted a look from Will to Rosie and back to Will again. 'Oh I see. Goodness me. Will and Penny Walsh! Well, well. Now that is news.' She met Rosie's furious glare. 'But ... why has this upset you? I assume from the way Penny's arm is linked through Will's they're much more than friends.'

'Apparently so.' Rosie's brows knit tighter together. 'It's been going on since before the New Year. He says he went to see how that Hermione Dunmore woman was coping after Stanley's funeral. She's the Walsh woman's sister.'

'Yes, I know. Hermione was staying with Penny at Sunnycliff Cottage for a time.'

'Yes. Well. He says that he and Penny...' Rosie shook herself dramatically. 'It makes me shudder to say her name.' She cleared her throat. 'That they discovered they have a lot of things in common. What those could be is beyond me. After Hermione left, he kept bumping into the woman and they joked about people thinking they'd arranged secret trysts. And then he said he realised he'd grown close to her since Christmas and that he would rather like to have a tryst with her, and it started from there. He says he's aware his parishioners might not approve, but he's given the matter considerable thought and he feels that love has been missing from his life for too many years. Well, we could all say that, couldn't we? I was astonished, as you can imagine.'

'Why? They're both single. They're around the same age. I don't know why they would need to keep it a secret though, and I can't see why you're so upset about it. If Will has finally found love with someone, surely you're happy for him? For them both. And they don't seem to be keeping it a secret now.'

'Precisely! But you're missing the point. He said he's been keeping their relationship quiet because he "knew how I would react" and he didn't want to cause me any unnecessary concern if it led to nothing.'

'I can understand that.'

Rosie tutted loudly. 'Well I can't! What does he mean by "knew how I would react"? Just because I can see how ridiculous such a relationship is and he can't, is that my problem? No. The fact that the entire village will be gossiping about him, doesn't seem to worry him. The woman doesn't believe in God! I told him in no uncertain terms that if he intends to bring her to live under our roof, I'm moving out!'

Stella gasped. 'Was that wise? Where will you live?'

'In Rosehip Cottage, of course. This won't last. He'll see the error of his ways once people start talking. He'll come round and end this farce. But I'm furious he's let it go this far. That he actually believes it's serious. That he hadn't even mentioned it until Friday evening, or discussed it with me. And where did he find the time to see her? He was no doubt sneaking off when I thought he was in his study working on his sermons.'

Stella sniggered. 'Good for him!'

'Good for him? There is nothing good about it. This isn't funny. When he said he intended to make their relationship public, once he'd informed me, I was horrified, Stella. Mortified! And I told him so. He had the audacity to tell me that, although he wasn't totally surprised by my reaction, he had hoped I would be happy for him. Then he asked me to keep his confidence for a few more days, until he and ... that woman, could discuss it further and decide how best to proceed. Is the man mad?'

Stella shook her head and squeezed Rosie's hand, giving Rosie a sympathetic smile.

'Oh, Rosie, Rosie, Rosie. Forgive me for saying this, but if anyone is mad in this scenario, it's you. What are we going to do with you?'

Chapter 15

Meeting Trisha was as bad as Iris had expected, but at least it was over with quickly, and the woman did smile at her when Bentley introduced them. It was shortly after Stella and Archer's speeches, and Iris and Elodie had gone to join Archer and Bentley. A second or two later, Trisha appeared from nowhere and called out Bentley's name.

'You're here!' Bentley said, clearly unable to contain his excitement as he kissed Trisha on the cheek. 'You look fantastic. I'm so pleased you came. I can't wait to show you the kitchen. You'll love it. But first, let me introduce you to everyone. This is Iris.'

'It's lovely to meet you,' Iris said, holding out her hand and then quickly withdrawing it because the somewhat formal gesture made her feel even more awkward than she already felt.

Admittedly Trisha's smile was a little icy, and it didn't seem to reach her eyes, but as her eyes were narrowed at the time, it was difficult to tell.

'Yes,' said Trisha, her cool grey eyes giving Iris a thorough once over. 'I thought it probably was. It's good to meet you too.' Trisha looked away and smiled warmly at Bentley. 'I seem to have mislaid my sunglasses.' Bentley gave her his, and proceeded to introduce her to Elodie and Archer.

Was that it?

Iris had hoped to exchange at least a couple of pleasantries with the woman. But she didn't really care. Instead, she beamed at Scott, ignoring the fact that Trisha was possibly the most beautiful woman she had seen for a while. And also, the rudest.

'You survived the storm then.' She was tempted to kiss him on the cheek as Bentley had Trisha, but he was standing farther away than Trisha had been and, knowing her luck, Iris would've overreached and fallen flat on her face.

'We barely noticed it,' he joked, winking at her. 'This is Ava,' he said, holding his daughter's hand, seemingly unaware of any tension between Iris and Trisha, and then he lowered his voice. 'You look lovely.'

'Thanks. You look pretty good too.' She smiled at Ava and crouched down so that their eyes were level. The little girl was the image of her dad apart from her cute, button nose and her golden curls. Those she had no doubt acquired from her mum, Veronica. She wore a pale purple dress, and in her hair, a matching, sparkly bow that sort of stood up like a miniature tiara. Iris couldn't image Scott tying that bow, for some reason. 'I'm very pleased to meet you, Ava. Your daddy didn't tell me you're a princess. Or are you incognito?'

'No. I'm Ava.' The little girl creased her tiny brows. 'I am a princess sometimes. And sometimes I'm a little monster. You've got pretty hair.'

'Thank you, Ava. Not as pretty as yours. I wish I had your golden curls.'

'That's what Daddy says.'

Scott rolled his eyes as Iris grinned up at him.

'Your daddy's got nice hair too.'

'Uh-huh.' Ava swung one foot back and forth across the grass. 'May I have a balloon? Please.' She looked up at Scott. 'I said please, Daddy.'

'I know you did, sweetheart. You're a very good girl. I'm sure we can find you a balloon.'

'Of course we can,' Iris said. 'There're lots of balloons inside.'

'A purp one?'

'She means purple,' Scott told Iris. 'She has trouble saying it.'

'I'm sure my friend Elodie can find you a purple one. Can't you, El?' Iris stood up and tugged at Elodie's sleeve.

Elodie had been chatting with Archer, Bentley and Trisha, who had seemed far friendlier to Elodie than she had to Iris.

'Sorry? What?' Elodie glanced round and smiled.

'This is Scott Fitzgerald, El, and his daughter, Ava. Ava would like a purple balloon. Do you have any purple ones? I'm sure you do.'

'Hi, Scott. Hello Ava. Yes we do. I saw some purple ones inside. Let's go in, shall we?'

Both Scott and Ava gave Elodie happy smiles. Iris wasn't sure which one of them was happiest. And then Scott pulled out a strip of purple rubber from his jeans pocket and whispered to Iris.

'I brought one of my own, just in case. Purple is Ava's favourite colour.'

'I'll make sure I remember that.'

'There's no need,' Trisha said, her voice low, almost as if only Iris was meant to hear that.

'After you,' Bentley said, standing aside to let Trisha pass.

Elodie followed right behind but Iris stopped beside Archer.

'This is Archer,' she said as Scott and Ava moved forward. 'Archer, please say Hi to Scott and his daughter Ava.'

Archer gave them a warm welcome. 'It's great to meet you both. Thanks for coming to our opening. I hear you're staying at The Lighthouse. I don't know if Iris has told you but Elodie and I live in The Bow and Quiver, the pub right opposite. We can wave to you from the windows.'

'Great to meet you too,' Scott said, with equal warmth. 'Iris did mention that. I was hoping to drop in on Sunday but the weather had other ideas.'

'That's the only problem with The Lighthouse,' Archer said, laughing. 'That, and all the stairs.'

'There are certainly a lot of stairs,' Scott agreed. 'And with Ava only having little legs, well, I don't think I thought it through.'

'I bet she loves it though,' Archer added. 'I know I did when I was young. Actually. I still do. There's something about a lighthouse.'

'Scott's novel is set at a lighthouse,' Iris said. 'I told you he's a writer.'

'Oh yeah.' Archer nodded. 'You did mention that once or twice.' He shot a cheeky smile at Iris and then returned his attention to Scott. 'That must be fun.'

Scott shook his head and smiled sardonically. 'Not as much as you might think. I've had a severe case of writer's block and I'm way behind schedule. That's why Trisha thought staying at The Lighthouse might help. But it's only since I met Iris, that the words are flowing again.'

Archer grinned. 'Iris has that effect on people.'

'I'm his muse.' Iris held her head high and stuck out her chin.

'What's a muse, Daddy?' Ava asked, shaking Scott's hand to get his attention.

'It's a person who inspires writers and other creative people like me. Someone who helps us think of ideas.'

'A nice person?' Ava looked thoughtful.

'A very nice person.' Scott smiled at Iris.

Archer raised his brows and laughed. 'Food and drinks are free this morning, so lots of coffee and chocolate cake may also help.'

'I'll try anything,' Scott said, laughing too. 'Thanks for letting us join in with your big day. And congratulations.'

Iris ushered Scott and Ava inside, where Elodie produced a giant, purple balloon, almost as big as Ava and handed it to Iris. It had the Cove Café Bistro logo on one side but the other side was plain.

'For you, Ava,' Iris said, smiling gratefully at Elodie before passing the balloon to Ava.

The expression on Ava's face was priceless, as if she had never seen anything quite as wonderful in her life, and she gave a squeal of delight, letting go of Scott's hand and holding the ribbon attached to the balloon, in both of hers.

'Thank you! May I keep it?'

Ava's delighted smile made Iris rather emotional. So much so that it took a second or two for her to reply.

'You're very welcome, Ava. And yes. It's yours to keep.'

Scott mouthed a thank you to both Elodie and Iris, looking almost as emotional as Iris felt.

'Bentley's saved one of the tables in the window for you,' Elodie said to Scott, pointing at the table before letting out a small sigh. 'He's currently boring Trisha to tears in the kitchen, but he'll let her join you shortly. Although to be fair, she did seem oddly keen to go and look at it.'

Scott laughed. 'That's because she's also a chef, and like all chefs, I presume, she finds kitchens fascinating.'

'Oh. I thought she was Ava's nanny.' Elodie looked confused.

'She is,' Scott confirmed. 'But it's only temporary, and she's doing me a favour. She lost her position as head chef when the restaurant where she worked closed down. She decided to take a break while she looked for something else, which worked out well for me, because Ava's school had just discovered asbestos in several rooms, so that had to shut down too.'

'Wow. Perfect timing.' Elodie smiled. 'I think either Iris or Bentley did mention that. Sorry. My brain is like mush right now what with today, the restaurant opening on Thursday, and the fact that Archer and I are off to Aus on Friday and we're not quite sure how long we'll be gone.'

Iris gasped. 'Don't tell me you've changed your minds again! You said it would be three months at the most.'

Elodie screwed up her face. 'Or thereabouts. Don't worry, Iris. I promise you we'll come back. But right now, you and I had better go and give Harley and Nina a hand.'

Iris scowled at Elodie. 'Fine. But if you're not back after three months I'm coming to get you.'

Elodie laughed, gave Scott and Ava a wave, and hurried towards the kitchen.

Iris shrugged, and smiled at Scott. 'This'll be the longest we've been apart since we were about five. Ava's age! We're more like sisters. Although El does have a sister. In Melbourne. She's one of the people El and Archer are going to visit. Anyway. Sorry but I've got to leave you and Ava to your own devices. Only Harley works here, and she's new, so El and I have been roped in to help out today. Thankfully, Nina – Harley's aunt, is also lending a hand. Oooh! You can be my first customers. What can I get you? Oh. You'd better take a seat first, I suppose. And maybe look at the menu. I'll go and get you one of those.'

With Scott's laughter ringing in her ears, Iris dashed off to find a menu.

Chapter 16

Stella lifted the lid of the laptop and stared at the blank screen, feeling more than a little confused. She knew how to turn the thing on, but she couldn't remember what to do after that.

'You okay there, Stella?' Iris asked, clearing a nearby table. 'Where's Rosie? Has she abandoned you?'

'I'm sorry, Iris. I was miles away. Rosie's gone to meet a plumber. Harley's father, actually. I have no idea if she'll be coming back. I'm waiting for Archer. He said he'd help me make a video call, or something, to Marian, but he's been so busy, and I think he may have forgotten because he seems to have left. I don't mind. I'm sure he'll show me later. I thought I might give it a try, but I'm at a total loss.' She closed the lid and smiled. 'Today has been a great success, hasn't it?'

'Giving away free food and drink is always popular, but yes. Everyone's really pleased. Apart from me. I'm just exhausted.' Iris grinned and winked. 'I don't think I've ever worked so hard in my life. I need a five-minute break.' She waved at Elodie, tapped her watch, held up her hand and spread her fingers. 'I'm taking five, El. Okay?' Elodie smiled and nodded in response, and Iris sat beside Stella. 'I can help you with this. Here. Let me show you.'

'Oh!' Stella was surprised. 'Are you sure? That's very kind.'

'Anything to get the weight off my feet,' Iris said, grinning again. 'I've been at it for over two hours. And I'm not even getting paid. Apart from in cake and coffee. Speaking of which.' She turned and whistled at Elodie, adding, 'Some service would be nice.'

'What can I get you?' Harley appeared at the table, smiling.

'Oh.' Iris looked embarrassed. 'I was joking, Harley. I can get it myself.'

'No, no. There's a bit of a lull. I'll be happy to get it for you. Coffee and chocolate cake? For two?'

'You can read my mind,' Iris said. 'Yes please.'

'Coming right up.'

'Not for me,' Stella said, too late. 'I've only just had breakfast.'

'That was more than two hours ago, Stella,' said Iris, opening the laptop and turning it on. 'And chocolate cake is a necessity when dealing with technology. Now watch and learn.'

Stella watched, but as for learning, she wasn't sure about that. Iris did explain what she was doing, and it did look very simple and straightforward, but Iris was so fast that before Stella had a chance to go over it in her mind, Marian's smiling face was on the screen.

'Hi, Marian,' Iris said. 'You really do look fantastic. Got any vacancies on that yacht? I've been slaving away in your café for the last two hours, so I do have some experience.' She laughed. 'But Stella's here, and I've got chocolate cake on the way, so I'll catch you later.' She waved and moved the laptop screen into a better position for Stella.

Marian was laughing. 'I'm sure we could find something for you, Iris. Speak soon. Hello again, Stella. So how was the reopening? I really wish I could've been there.'

Stella beamed at Iris, who nodded, flopped back against her seat and closed her eyes.

'It was a complete success,' Stella said. 'Harley, Nina, Elodie and Iris have all been rushed off their feet. Not forgetting Archer and Bentley. I believe everyone in the village has popped in. They've all said how much you're missed but those who saw you on the screen earlier all agreed how wonderful you look and how they're sure you made the right decision. And you did, Marian. So I hope you don't have any feelings of regret, or guilt, or any such nonsense.'

'You know me so well,' Marian said, looking slightly tearful. 'I don't have any regrets, as such, but I do feel a little guilty sometimes about leaving you. Especially after everything you've done for me. I know you said I mustn't, but we're only human, aren't we?'

'We are, my darling, but as I told you when you left, and each time we've spoken on the phone since, there is nothing to feel guilty about. Your happiness means the world to me and knowing you're happy, makes me happy. And now I can tell you so face to face, at least once or twice a week, thanks to this marvellous gift. Although I promise I won't pester you and become a nuisance.'

'You could never be a nuisance, Stella. You've be a second mum to me and I'll love you forever for that. Ah, I can see the chocolate cake is coming. Parker wanted to say hi but he's on the phone with his dad, so shall we catch up again later? I know you don't have internet access at home but the pub does. Let Archer know what time is good for you and we'll set something up. Is that okay with you?'

'Of course it is.'

'Bye for now then. And bye, Iris,' Marian said.

Iris sat upright and smiled. 'Bye Marian. See you around. Don't have too much fun.' She turned off the laptop a few seconds later.

Stella let out a sigh. She had been looking forward to a long chat with Marian but clearly it wasn't to be. And Archer would be busy all day. She couldn't bother him.

'Two slices of chocolate cake and two coffees. Enjoy.' Harley placed the food and drinks on the table, smiled and went to take a new order.

'Thanks, Harley,' Iris said, before glancing at Stella. 'You okay, Stella?'

Stella nodded. 'Yes. A little emotional, that's all. Thank you for doing that, Iris.'

'Anytime. But you look like I feel. Disappointed.'

Stella sucked in a breath. 'Disappointed? What makes you say that? And more importantly, why are you disappointed? The cake looks delicious.'

'It's not the cake. Cake never disappoints.'

'What is it then? From what I've seen and heard, you've met a lovely young man, and Bentley's rekindled an old flame. Ah. Is that why? You've realised that you do, in fact, have feelings for Bentley, but now he might be dating someone else.'

'What? No. But boy, does word travel fast in this village.' Iris shook her head and dug her pastry fork into her cake. 'It's no wonder Stanley knew everything about everyone, and was able to acquire such a mountain of information.'

Stella had tried to forget about Stanley Talbot.

'Secrets are hard to keep in Clementine Cove, my dear, it's true. But your uncle didn't know everything. He thought he did, I'm sure. But he was wrong.'

'Really?' Iris studied Stella over a forkful of cake hovering just below Iris' chin. 'That sounds as if there was something he didn't know about you, Stella Pinkheart. What deep, dark secrets were you able to hide from him?' Iris grinned and popped the cake into her mouth.

'Nothing worth talking about. Why then, are you disappointed? If it's not the cake, and it's not Bentley ... are things not going well with Scott? You young people are always in such a rush. You need to give it time, Iris. You've only just met, after all. I must say Ava is a delight. Such perfect manners and so pretty too. You do like children, don't you?'

Iris raised her brows. 'Not as much as I like chocolate cake. But they're okay. Ava's great. You're right. But I haven't spent much time around kids so I'm not sure what to do or say. And Trisha is clearly not my biggest fan, so there's that. As for being in a rush, he's only here for a month. It might just be a holiday thing – not fling. Thing. But I hope it's something more. And before you ask, yes, there's a difference. Flings don't involve feelings. Things do – but they don't last.'

'I wasn't going to ask. As it happens, I understand that. But I still don't see why you're disappointed. I can see why you might be unsure of yourself, and of the situation, but I don't think there's any need to be. As I said, give it time. And you seem to be doing very well with Ava. I wouldn't worry about that. The nanny, however. Hmmm. That's a different kettle of fish.'

'She disliked me before we met, and I'm not sure why. Surely the fact that what Bentley and I had wasn't serious, and was just about sex, is a good thing? No one got hurt and no one was in love.'

'Perhaps it's not about Bentley, it just seems as if it is. Perhaps it's about Scott and Ava.'

'Yeah. That's partly it. Scott's wife was Trisha's best friend, so Trisha's very protective of Ava and Scott. She wants him to find 'the perfect woman', but perfect women don't exist. She's got the impression that I'm far from perfect, and I think she's worried I'll mess Scott around and end up hurting him and Ava. Which I won't. I expect you agree with her, don't you?'

'Actually, no. And I think it may be more than that, but we'll have to wait and see. I do agree that you don't seem to take life seriously. And sex seems very important to you, but there's nothing wrong with that. I believe that beneath the mask you show to most of us, is a deeply caring, loving and loyal woman who wants to find the right man, just as her best friend has done. Ah. Is that the disappointment? The fact that Elodie is leaving earlier than expected and will be away for longer than first planned?'

Iris grinned at her. 'You're good, Stella. You see everything, don't you? But the reason I'm disappointed right now is actually because I was hoping to go out on a date with Scott tonight, and now we can't.'

'Why not?'

'Because Trisha has already made plans with Bentley. She told Scott she's happy to cancel them, but he says he can't ask her to do that. We can't go out tomorrow night because I promised El I'd be around to help out here, along with Bentley. There's still so much to do for the restaurant opening on

Thursday, and El and Archer have got loads of other stuff to do, not least, to run the pub. So I won't ask her if I can duck out.' Iris shrugged. 'We'll have to wait until Friday, I suppose. And I know you'll say that's not a big deal and I'm rushing things again, but Scott's also got his book to write, so time is limited. Plus he needs, sorry, wants to spend time with Ava, too. Obviously.'

'I see.'

Iris drained her coffee and gathered the empty plates. 'And now I've got to get back to work. But first, I want to know why you looked disappointed.'

Stella waved her hand in the air. 'Just an old woman being foolish.'

'I've told you everything, Stella. Play fair.'

Stella looked Iris in the eye. 'I was simply hoping for a longer conversation with Marian, that's all. You've just said yourself how busy Archer is. I can't bother him with this.' She pointed to the laptop. 'Especially as it was such a kind and thoughtful gift. And I'm so grateful to you for just now, Iris. That meant a lot to me. But although you made it all look so easy, I'm not sure I could manage on my own. Plus there's the issue with the WiFi. I don't have an internet connection at home.'

Iris tutted. 'How do you survive?' And then she laughed. 'That's easily solved. Now you've got this laptop you're going to need to get that sorted. You could come here, or go to the pub, or anywhere else with a connection, but if the weather's crap, the last thing you need is to have to go out. If you're happy to hang around here, we'll search for the best provider for what you want and we'll get that booked during my next break. It'll take a week or two to get it up and running, but in the meantime, just give me a shout. Or even Rosie. I'm sure she's on the internet. She'll know what to do. Or I'll show her. And you tell me what time you want to call Marian again today, and I'll be here. Or wherever. The pub would be good.'

'That ... that all sounds wonderful. Are you sure you don't mind?'

'Not at all. You've got my number, haven't you?'

'Er. No. I haven't.'

'That's also easily remedied. Give me your phone and I'll add myself to your contacts.'

Chapter 17

Rosie opened the front door of Rosehip Cottage and had to stifle a gasp. She had not expected this! All the plumbers she had ever seen (admittedly not that many, but ten or twelve, perhaps) had all been short and fat, or tall and hairy, or unable to dress themselves properly, having jeans showing half their bottoms – and not in a good way. This man was nothing short of angelic. In looks at least.

'You must be Pete.'

'Must I?'

His smile was slightly devilish and the twinkle in his baby blue eyes was something else entirely. She glanced past him towards the, surprisingly white, van with Pete's Plumbing emblazoned along the side.

'Aren't you?'

'Afraid not, love. Close. But no banana. I'm Joe. Joe Davissen. But I am Harley's dad.'

Rosie tutted. No banana? Did the man think that was funny? And then it dawned on her.

'Davidson? Good grief. Harley Davidson as in *Harley-Davidson*!'

'Wrong again. Davissen.' He grinned. 'But yeah. We did call her Harley because her mum and I both had Harleys when we met. I've still got my bike. And Harley. But her mum is long gone. Ran off with a stock car driver.' He nodded to his van. 'Pete's my dad. I haven't got around to changing the logo on the van, and besides, Pete's Plumbing has a good reputation. Silly to risk confusing customers by changing the name. Didn't Harley tell you?'

'No. She didn't.'

'Oh well.' The grin broadened. 'I'm a pretty good plumber, love, but even I can't fix a shower unless I'm somewhere near it. Are you going to let me in?'

'Yes. Sorry. I'm a little confused.'

Rosie stood to one side and closed the door behind him as he stepped into the hall.

'Happens to us all, love, at our age.'

'I beg your pardon!'

'No need to apologise. Just show me the way to your shower.'

'Apologise! I was *not* apologising. I was expressing my astonishment at your audacity.'

'Yeah. I get that a lot. But I've never heard it called audacity before.'

He winked at her and she almost choked on her gasp of surprise.

'This way, is it?' he continued. 'Harley said it's the one in your en suite. I'm assuming it's upstairs.'

She managed to regain some composure. 'I'll lead the way if you don't mind.'

'I don't mind at all, love.'

He didn't move out of her way and she had to squeeze past him; his aftershave pervaded her nostrils and his warm breath on her cheek sent odd shivers down her spine.

'Please stop calling me 'love'. I find it offensive. My name is Miss Parker. Or Rosamunde.'

'You find love offensive? Righty-oh, Rosamunde.'

He said her name very slowly. Annoyingly so, in fact. She glowered at him.

'I don't find love offensive. I find the word offensive when used by a complete stranger.'

'Not a believer in love at first sight then, Rosamunde?'

'Love at...? No! Absolutely not.'

'Me neither. Harley's mum is and so is Harley. So's my sister, Nina. But you and me. We know better, don't we, Rosamunde?'

'Follow me,' she said, ignoring that remark.

'To the moon and back.'

She could hear the laughter in his voice, but again, chose to ignore the comment.

Was he always this rude? This irritating?

If he hadn't been Harley's father, she would've sent him packing.

In fact, she still might.

But then again, she did need her shower repaired.

She could feel his eyes on her as she took him to her bedroom. Never in her wildest dreams would she be interested in such a man – and yet – knowing he was watching her every move made her feel ... sexy. Powerful. Invigorated. Sensual.

What was wrong with her?

The man was a plumber, for Heaven's sake. Rosie did not date tradesmen.

'This is my bedroom.'

He looked around the room and then met her eyes.

'It's you to a tee.'

'You know nothing about me.'

'Wrong again. I know a lot about you ... Rosie.'

'Only my friends call me Rosie.'

'We'll be friends by the time I've fixed your shower. Any chance of a cuppa? Strong and sweet, please. Just like you.'

Rosie couldn't believe her ears.

'Does this ever work?'

He raised his brows. 'What?'

'This ... this chat up game, or whatever it is.'

He shrugged. 'I'm not trying to chat you up. Or play games. Is that what you think?'

'You behave like this to all your new customers, do you?'

'More or less. Yes. This is who I am. Take me or leave me.'

'I'll leave you. The shower is in there.' She pointed to the en suite. 'I'll be downstairs. Try not to touch anything you don't need to.'

He grinned, much to her surprise, but as she left the room he said, 'Two sugars, please. And if you've got a biscuit, that would go down a treat. I skipped lunch so that I could fit you in and I'm feeling a bit peckish.'

Chapter 18

Rosie made her way to the table in the window of Cove Café Bistro and sat on the seat she had vacated more than three hours earlier.

'I can't believe you're still here,' she said to Stella, looking around the café in disbelief. 'At least it's much quieter than it was this morning. I suppose that's because the food and drinks are no longer free.'

'You're such a cynic, Rosie.' Stella shook her head and sighed.

'I'm a realist. Why couldn't we meet in the pub? I need a stiff drink after the experience I've just had.'

'Because I don't want Archer to see me and to think I'm trying to remind him he was going to help me with this laptop.' She patted the closed laptop that sat on the table in front of her. 'Although Iris has been wonderful.

But if I mention that to Archer, he might feel guilty and I wouldn't want that.'

Rosie took a deep breath. 'I have no idea what any of that meant. But this is far more important.' She leant forward and glanced towards the kitchen. 'I've spent the last forty minutes with Harley's father. And I have to tell you, he's odd, to put it mildly. But annoyingly, he's also rather attractive. If you like that sort of thing. Which of course, I don't. I definitely do not.' She shuddered dramatically. 'He tried to hit on me. He says he wasn't, but he was. I'm not stupid. I can tell when a man is attracted to me. You can see it in their eyes.'

'Can you?' Stella seemed surprised. 'It's been so long since any man has even looked at me, so I'll have to take your word for that.'

'Men look at me all the time. Especially when I'm running. It's the figure-hugging Lycra. And even if I say so myself, I do still have a good body.'

Stella coughed. 'And you do often say so. Did he ask you out? But I suppose, more importantly, is your shower repaired?'

Rosie tutted. 'You can be a mean old biddy sometimes, Stella Pinkheart. No he didn't. Not in so many words. But if I'd shown the slightest interest – which I didn't – he would've done so, I'm sure of that. And yes. It appears my shower is now as good as new. Better, in fact, I have to admit.'

'Then you should thank Harley for asking him to pop round.'

'I intend to. Ah. There she is. Are we having lunch here?'

'I'm not hungry. I've had breakfast and chocolate cake. I couldn't eat a thing.'

'I'm ravenous. I'm going to have a large, mixed salad.' She waved to Harley who waved back and smiled as she approached the table.

'Dad's just called,' Harley said, before Rosie had a chance to speak. 'He says it was great to finally meet you in the flesh. And he's looking forward to seeing more of you.'

From Harley's lips, those words sounded innocent and friendly, but Rosie could hear Joe Davissen's voice and see the look in those baby blue eyes and suddenly the words had an entirely different connotation. Rosie had to bite back a squeal of excitement and she wasn't sure what shocked her the most. That she was suddenly the type of woman who would actually squeal. Or that something Joe Davissen said could make her feel so excited.

She must be going through the change. Or maybe she was unwell. Those were the only two rational explanations.

'Rosamunde! Harley is speaking to you.'

Rosie stared at Stella. 'What? Oh goodness. I'm so sorry, Harley. My mind was elsewhere for a moment. Thank you so much for getting your father to fit me in today. He's done an excellent job. So good, in fact, that I've suggested to my brother that we should ask Joe ... I mean, Mr Davissen, to carry out a thorough check of all our plumbing and central heating. Just in case.'

'Yes. He's just told me that he'll be doing more work for you and your brother. What can I get you?'

'Get me? Oh. My order. A large, mixed salad, please. And maybe a portion of French fries. I feel like being naughty.'

Stella rolled her eyes when Harley walked away.

'What is wrong with you today? You're behaving like a teenager.'

'No I'm not! Shush. Here comes Iris. If anyone is behaving like ... Hello, Iris. How are you?'

'I'm okay thanks. You're looking a little flushed, Rosie. What's made you so happy?'

'Her plumber,' Stella said.

Rosie tutted. 'What Stella means is that I've just had my shower repaired after days of it not working properly.'

'That's good. It's the little things in life that make us smile. I've tried to show Stella how to make a video call to Marian but I think I went too fast so I'll need to show her again later. I was wondering though if you're good with technology. We've booked to have internet connected at Pinkheart Cottage, so it would be great to know that Stella will have someone else to ask for help if I'm not around. Archer and El would, but they'll be gone on Friday, and Bentley won't have a second to himself.'

'They're off on Friday? I believe I did hear Archer mention that. Why did they bring their trip forward?'

'Convenience, I believe. So yes or no?'

'Oh. Er. Wait.' Rosie met Stella's eyes. 'You're getting WiFi! Have the four horsemen been informed? Is this the end of the world as we know it? Why the sudden rush to join this century?'

'Amusing as ever, Rosamunde. Will you help me or not?'

'Of course I'll help you. Don't I always?'

Stella raised her brows but didn't respond and Iris patted Rosie on the arm and smiled.

'That's brilliant. And I've had a thought, Stella. As I won't be going out on my date, why don't you come to my place this evening? We can call Marian from there, and I can show you lots of other cool stuff on the internet. We should get you on social media. I'll take something from here that Bentley's cooked and heat it up. And then I'll walk you back to your cottage and go for a quick drink in the pub. You're welcome to come for a drink, of course, but you might be tired by then.'

'I can't ask you to do all that, Iris,' Stella said, sounding genuinely moved.

'You didn't. I offered. And it's no big deal. I could use the company.'

'Your date's been cancelled?' Rosie queried. 'With Bentley? Or the new man?'

'The new man.' Iris pulled a face. 'His name is Scott.'

'Why did he cancel?'

'He didn't. Exactly. The nanny had already made other plans.'

'With Bentley? We reap what we sow, Iris.'

'Thanks. I'll bear that in mind. If I ever understand it. What do you say, Stella?'

'I say, thank you very much. I'd be delighted.'

'I'm surprised you didn't ask Stella to step in and babysit,' Rosie said, smiling when Iris and Stella exchanged glances.

'Why didn't I think of that?' Stella asked.

Iris shook her head, looking slightly bewildered. 'I don't think Scott would agree to it. I realise you'd be the perfect person, but he doesn't know you from Adam. And what if something happened? I'd never forgive myself.'

'No. Neither would I.'

'What could possibly happen?' Rosie said, getting a little frustrated.

'A lot,' said Iris. 'And what about the tides? Stella might have to spend the night at The Lighthouse.'

'Or Stella could babysit at your cottage. I assume your plan was to have Scott spend the night.' Rosie rolled her eyes. 'He could take the child there. You could all have supper together. Then you and he could go out for a shorter date than planned. Stella could return home once you're back, and the child would be fast asleep so none the wiser. It would be an adventure for her, I shouldn't wonder. I know you'll ensure Scott has a lovely time, so you'll have no complaints from him. And if he gets up before the child awakes, she won't know where her father slept. Or didn't sleep, as the case may be.' Rosie let out a sigh.

'Wow, Rosie,' Iris laughed. 'That is some plan. Did you really just think that all up?'

'No. I read it in one of my brother's sermons. Obviously, I thought it up. What surprises me, is why you didn't.'

'I wonder if Scott will agree to it,' Stella said. 'I'll happily play my part.'

'No.' Iris shook her head. 'I invited you round for the evening to show you how to use the internet, not to babysit.'

'You can show me before he arrives. Or another time. I would like to have a chat with Marian this evening, but other than that it can all wait. Honestly, Iris. If Scott agrees, I'm more than happy.'

'I think Trisha may have something to say about it.' Iris looked deflated.

'She's the nanny?' Rosie checked.

'Yes. And she's not a fan. And not just because I've been having sex with Bentley. I really need to get her to like me.'

'Why?'

Both Stella and Iris stared at Rosie.

'Because the woman is like a second mum to Scott's child, Ava. And because she was the mum's best friend. She's Scott's friend too. Both Scott and Ava will compare me to her, I know they will. And if she doesn't like me, they might think I'm not a good fit.'

Stella nodded. 'You need to show Scott and Ava – and Trisha too, that you're not trying to replace Trisha. That you want her to remain a part of the family if this relationship goes anywhere.'

Iris curled her lip. 'Do I though? Have you seen how stunning she is? What is wrong with me? Of course I do. She'll be with Bentley. So we'll all be friends together.'

'How delightful,' Rosie said. 'But you're forgetting the dead wife. If Scott is going to be comparing you with anyone, it'll be with her.'

Iris' shoulders hunched. 'Thanks, Rosie. I hadn't even considered that.'

'I'm here to help,' Rosie said. 'I almost wish I could tag along, but sadly I have plans for this evening.'

She tried to ignore the fact that she hadn't been asked. And she definitely wasn't going to tell them her plans involved shutting herself in her bedroom, with a bottle of red wine, staring at her 32-inch desktop screen, signed in to one of the five online interactive live casinos of which she was a member. She would be playing roulette and also taking part in a Poker tournament, trying to recoup some of the money she had lost over the last few nights.

She still blamed her brother's news for her change of fortune. She had been doing extremely well for the past few months. So well that she'd been able to buy her gorgeous new watch. A watch that she may have to sell if things didn't turn around in her favour soon.

She prided herself on the fact that she had always stayed within her set limits but all that had gone out of the window lately. A few exceedingly big wins had made her over confident, but on Friday night, she'd almost doubled her usual spend after losing one game after another. Saturday was even worse. Sunday was a disaster. That was the problem with gambling, especially from the comfort of one's own room, and online gambling was addictive. Vast sums of money could be won, or lost, in an instant.

But tonight would be the night. She would have one final splurge. Her luck had turned, she could feel it. Her shower was fixed; her bank balance would soon be back in the black. And then she would ensure she stuck within her own set limits.

Chapter 19

Iris was thrilled. When she phoned Scott to tell him about Rosie's plan (without mentioning that it was Rosie's plan) he thought it was a great idea.

'Stella is a pillar of the local community, and a retired school teacher. And you won't believe this, but she taught children between the ages of five and six. So she's the perfect babysitter.'

'Child carer, we like to call it,' Scott jovially corrected her. 'Ava doesn't consider herself a baby, and she's right, of course. But she never really has. As soon as she understood what a baby was, she made it clear she had outgrown that. And as Trisha was usually my child carer, I don't think I ever used the word babysitter. And Stella is a lifesaver, if this means we can go on our date.'

'Child carer it is then. So you're happy to bring Ava here, and for you both to stay the night, along with Stella? There's no pressure for you to spend the night with me. Unless you want to. The cottage only has three bedrooms but one of the beds separates into two singles, so you and Ava could have that room, if you like.'

'That sounds good. But let's see how the date goes, shall we? Although I think I know where I'll be sleeping. Unless you decide otherwise.'

'That's as good as settled. What time does Ava go to bed? Only I promised to set up a video call for Stella and a friend, and then I want to show her how to use the internet. She's great with kids but not with technology. Oh, and what time do you usually eat?'

'Ava could probably show her how to do that,' Scott said, cheerily. 'As for meal and bed times, we eat around 6-ish and Ava's in bed between 7 and 8 p.m. but it's closer to 8 since she's been homeschooled.'

'Let's say we'll eat at 6 then, so if you get here around 5.45 that would be perfect. We can play games or something until Ava's in bed and then we can go to the pub, or for a walk, or whatever, knowing she'll be safe with Stella.'

'I can't wait,' he said, his tone emphasising the fact.

'Neither can I,' said Iris, as seductively as she could.

She then spent half an hour asking Elodie, Harley and Nina what they thought she should wear; casual or sexy, finally deciding on a combination of both. Smart but casual trousers with a sexy, clingy top, covered by a cardigan or jumper until Ava went to bed and then cast aside when she was alone with Scott.

After that she pestered Bentley for something suitable for a five-year-old to eat, and a seventy-five-year-old, but also sophisticated enough for a date night.

'I want it to seem as though we're all eating the same meal, but I want it to be quick and easy, and not too fussy for Ava, yet tasty and interesting for Stella, and sophisticated and sexy for me and Scott.'

'And you want this within the hour?'

'Or less, if possible. I need to get home, showered and dressed and show Stella how to make video calls and do some general stuff online.'

'Burgers,' he eventually said.

'No need to swear,' she joked. 'Oh. Burgers. Remind me again how they fall under the sophisticated and sexy banner.'

'I'll remind you that I've got a date of my own tonight, plus a thousand things to get done here before that, and you can tell me if you'd like burgers or bugger all. Your choice.'

'Burgers it is then.'

'Good choice. Add peas and chips for the kid. And no doubt, ordinary tomato ketchup.' He shuddered. 'Add peas and maybe asparagus for Stella, without any chips or sauces or she'll probably end up with indigestion. But ask her. I'll make sure their burgers are simple but tasty. Keep theirs separate from yours. Add a mushroom and brandy sauce for you and Scott, with petit pois, butter roasted asparagus and French fries. You see. Change a few words and add some alcohol and you've got sexy and sophisticated. Or as close as you're going to get in the time I've got to spare. I'll give you everything you'll need, including oven timings.'

'You're a star, Bentley. I hope you get lucky tonight.'

'I hope I can stay awake. I'm absolutely shattered.'

Iris left him in peace, after he packed up everything she would need and she'd typed the instructions and timings into her phone. She put it all in the boot of her car and went to pick up Stella who had popped home to get changed and collect her overnight bag.

'I'll set up the call with you and Marian and then I'll jump in the shower, get dressed and start preparing dinner. After that I think we should set you up on some social networking sites. You'll have fun with those once you know how they work. You could catch up with some old friends. Oh. I don't mean old as in ... old. I mean old as in friends you haven't seen for a long time.'

'I am old, Iris, and there's no point in pretending otherwise. As for this social media, I'm not sure about that. I think the past is best left where it is: in the past.'

'Oh come on, Stella. Are you seriously telling me that there aren't any old flames you'd like to catch up with? No old loves you'd like to discover have fallen flat on their faces, or, maybe, reached the heady heights of success?'

Stella gave an odd little cough. 'No. None.'

Iris stopped at a junction and stared at her. 'I can tell from your tone and your reaction that I've hit a nerve. Is this one of those deep, dark secrets that Stanley didn't know about you, Stella? Do you have a secret love somewhere in your past?'

'No, Iris! Now can we please drop the subject!'

Stella was evidently upset, and now Iris was eager to find out about Stella's past.

Because Iris was absolutely certain that somewhere out there was a man – or maybe a woman, with whom Stella Pinkheart was once in love. Deeply in love, judging by Stella's reaction. Assuming he or she was still alive.

Iris decided she should change the subject for now.

'Today was brilliant, wasn't it? Harley could never take Marian's place, but I think she's going to be fantastic, don't you? And what about Nina, her aunt? She's lovely, isn't she? So friendly and so calm. Did you see how she managed to get Bentley to stop and take a breath on more than one occasion? No, of course you didn't. That was in the kitchen. But she was great. Apparently, Trisha offered to lend a hand, but Bentley told her we'd got it covered. I'm glad he did. I don't think it would've been quite so much fun with Trisha lurking around.'

Stella was clearly deep in thought and didn't say a word, making Iris even more determined to find out all she could about Stella's past. Maybe Rosie knew. Iris would have to ask her.

Iris pulled up on the driveway.

'We're here, Stella.'

'Good gracious. I think I nodded off. I'm so sorry.'

'No apology necessary.' And now Stella was lying. Iris had definitely hit a nerve. 'I hope I don't have that effect on Scott tonight.'

Stella laughed. 'You won't, my dear. I'll help you with the boxes. I do love Bentley's burgers. I don't have them often so this is a real treat.'

Iris had told Stella what they were having when she'd picked her up. Bentley was right. No chips, or the grown up version, French fries, and no sauces.

'I can manage, if you don't mind grabbing your bag.'

Stella took her overnight bag from the boot and also picked up a couple of the containers of food and followed Iris inside. After depositing the containers in the kitchen, Iris took Stella to one of the guest bedrooms and then back downstairs to the study.

'I'll put the kettle on and make some tea and then we'll call Marian from here.'

Her laptop sat at the centre of Stanley's antique desk which had once been positioned in the middle of the room. Iris had moved the desk, and Stanley's red leather and oak, captain's chair, closer to the window, leaving enough space to access the window seat without banging into either. The shelves and racks, the pens in pots and the single plant were as they had been when Iris and Elodie had first moved in, but now several of Iris' books and ornaments sat on the shelves. Even the three old wooden filing cabinets to one side of the room remained in place. Although now they contained details of Iris' clients, and not people's secrets.

'Shall I light the log burning stove?' Iris asked when she returned with the tea. 'It feels a bit chilly in here. Perhaps I'll just turn the heating up and make sure the whole place feels warm and cosy and I'll light the wood burner in the sitting room instead.'

'Don't worry on my account,' said Stella. 'I'm warm enough. But a log fire does add an ambience to a room so I'd agree it's a good idea to have the one in the sitting room nice and toasty. I can do that when you're preparing dinner.'

'Great. Thank you. Let's call Marian then.'

Iris took Stella through the motions once again and stayed long enough to say hi to Marian and Parker before leaving Stella to it and dashing to the shower.

It took her longer than she'd hoped to get dressed, mainly because she changed her mind about which top to wear and tried on several before returning to her original choice. But she still had time to show Stella a few of the social media sites and to pique her interest.

'You see,' she said. 'I told you they'd be fun. Shall we set you up on one or two?'

'Perhaps just one. For now. Whichever one you think is the most popular for my age group.'

Iris helped Stella complete her profile on the site and showed her how to search for people, or groups, or places.

'Let's search for Cove Café Bistro,' Iris said, typing it into the search box. 'I know Bentley's made sure it's everywhere. And here it is.'

She clicked on it and smiled as the cover photo for the page was a photo from today, of the crowd and the reopening with Stella front and centre and the TV screen with Marian clearly visible behind. Archer and Bentley stood either side of Stella and Iris realised Elodie must've taken the photo from among the crowd.

'My goodness!'

Stella was overcome with emotion and Iris handed her a tissue.

'You're famous, Stella. And now we can even tag you in the photo. I'll show you how to do that.'

Iris scrolled through the recent posts, several of which had photos of the café and the refurbishment being carried out. Some had photos of Bentley and Archer. There was even one of Bentley and Iris that she couldn't recall being taken. Other posts had proposed menus for the café and the restaurant, and the pinned post gave details of Thursday's opening of the restaurant.

'Is The Bow and Quiver on here?' Stella asked, now obviously fascinated by the wonders of social media.

'Yep.'

Iris let Stella search for it and Stella gave a little squeal when she clicked on the relevant page. Stella scrolled through the posts Archer and Elodie had added recently and her excitement was building, that was quite clear.

'I'm going to search for The Lighthouse,' Stella said. 'Just because I want to be nosy and see how much Cordelia and Charles charge for the place.'

'I'd quite like to see that myself.'

They were both surprised and disappointed. The starting rate was high enough, but to get an accurate price, you had to input your dates and party size and when they tried to do that, a landing page appeared stating Cordelia and Charles were very sorry but The Lighthouse was now fully booked until the following year. There was a waiting list for a cancellation but there was no point in them following the link for that, so instead they scrolled through the posts and then they went back and clicked on the link to the main website to see if that gave detailed prices.

'Oh look!' Stella said. 'They feature various businesses and places of interest in Clementine Cove. That's a nice touch. It gives prospective visitors a taste of what the village has to offer during their stay. The Bow and Quiver's on here.'

Iris stared at the photo and a strange feeling fluttered in her stomach but she wasn't sure why. Archer looked as handsome as ever and Bentley did too. Bentley's chef's hat was cocked at a slight angle but it was bright white as was his apron with The Bow and Quiver emblazoned on the front.

'That's an old photo,' Iris said. 'The new logo for the pub is the same colour as the logo for Cove Café and Bistro. They wanted everyone to know the businesses were linked.'

'That's interesting. Didn't someone say that it was Trisha who found The Lighthouse on the internet? She must've been surprised to see the man she'd loved and lost standing outside of a pub that sits directly opposite.'

'Actually, Stella, that's more than interesting. It's odd. I heard that she had no idea Bentley lived in Clementine Cove and that it was obviously fate that brought her here. I was disappointed because Scott and I thought fate had brought him here to meet me. Sort of.'

'I don't understand. Why would she say that, when the first photo on the website, other than the banner photo as you called it, is of the pub, and Bentley and Archer's faces are as clear as day? Unless Bentley has changed so much that Trisha didn't recognise him.'

Iris shook her head. 'Nope. He showed me a photo he's had all these years of him and Trisha. She's changed a bit but you'd still know it was her. Bentley hasn't changed at all. Not one bit. Other than, perhaps, he's got a couple of wrinkles now. But even his hair is still the same. I actually made a joke about it. I asked how much virgins' blood he needed to drink every night to stay exactly as he was seventeen years or so ago. So you're right. Why would Trisha say she didn't know Bentley was here? And was that why she persuaded Scott to come? Or was it just a happy coincidence?'

'Perhaps she was worried Bentley might think she had been stalking him online or some such thing. I've heard about that happening. And I can now see, from looking at those social media sites, just how easy it is to do.'

'It isn't that easy. Not if someone's personal profile is set to private, or friends only. But Bentley's isn't. I may be overreacting but why do I get the feeling that Trisha may be hiding something?'

'I happen to agree with you. I was watching her today while she was in the café and I had the strangest feeling that all was not as it seemed. I believe I said as much when you kindly made that video call to Marian during your break.'

'Did you?'

Stella nodded. 'Yes. My memory isn't as good as it once was but I do still recall certain things with amazing accuracy. I believe it was when you said that Trisha didn't like you and you thought it was because of your previous 'friends with benefits' situation with Bentley. I told you that perhaps it's not about Bentley, it just seems as if it is. Perhaps it's about Scott and Ava and I thought it might be more than that, but we'd have to wait and see.'

'Oh yes. I remember that. But I wasn't sure what you meant then, and I'm still not.'

Stella shrugged. 'Simply that I think there is more going on than we realise and the truth will out, as they say. But the time is ticking on. We'd better get off this internet and get ready for Scott and Ava's arrival or you'll be running late. And tardiness is not the impression one wants to make on a first date.'

Chapter 20

Iris didn't know Scott well – hardly at all, in fact, but from the moment she opened her front door and stood aside to let him and Ava enter, she could tell that there was something wrong. For starters, it was gone 6 and he was supposed to arrive twenty minutes earlier. Stella was right. Tardiness was not a good impression on a first date.

'Hello,' she said, with an excited and relieved smile. She was considering texting him to see where he was just a minute before he rang the bell. 'It's lovely to see you again Ava. And you've brought your balloon! How wonderful. We'll tie that somewhere safe, shall we?'

'Yes please. I don't want to lose it.'

'Hi Scott. It's lovely to see you again too. I was beginning to think you'd changed your mind. Is everything okay? You look a little … frazzled.'

Scott shook his head and breathed out a sigh as if he'd been holding it in for some time.

'Sorry. I should've texted when we were on our way. There was a … an issue. I'll tell you about it later. Right now I need a glass of something alcoholic, please. And sorry again. It's great to see you. You look lovely.'

'You're here now. That's all that matters. Come in.'

She indicated the direction of the sitting room and Ava and Scott went ahead of her, hand-in-hand.

'Hello,' Scott said, on seeing Stella.

'This is Stella,' Iris said. 'Ava, Stella is a friend of mine and she was once a school teacher who taught children of your age. Stella, this is Ava and this is Scott.'

'Hello,' Ava said, looking a little nervous. She had one finger to her lips, with the balloon wrapped around that hand and she still held Scott's hand with the other.

'Hello, Ava and Scott,' Stella said, getting to her feet. 'My word, that's a splendid balloon. You're a very lucky girl. And a very pretty one. Did Daddy tie that bow in your hair?'

Ava shook her head from side to side, her finger still in place. 'No. Trisha did it. She's my friend. And Daddy's too.'

'That's nice. It's good to have friends. And balloons. It's always good to have a balloon. Would you like to come and sit by me and tell me about some of the other things you like?'

Ava darted a look up at Scott, who smiled. 'Would you like to do that, sweetheart? Stella is very nice.'

Ava nodded and let go of Scott's hand but as she made her way to Stella, she glanced back at Scott and at Iris.

Iris was pouring Scott a large glass of red wine from the bottle she had opened. Something caught in her throat as she watched Ava's hand slip into Stella's.

'Isn't the fire lovely and warm?' Stella said, 'But we mustn't sit too close to it. Would you like to sit on my lap, or in this big chair nearby?'

'Your lap. Please.'

Scott took the glass from Iris and he beamed at her. 'I told Trisha there was no need to worry.' He took a large mouthful and when he had swallowed, he let out another sigh.

'Was Trisha worried? Is that why you were late?'

Scott shook his head. 'Yeah. And it was all so silly. But I don't want Ava to hear.'

'Come into the kitchen with me,' Iris said. 'Ava will be fine with Stella.'

Scott looked uncertain but Ava was chattering away about ponies and foxes and all sorts of things, so he said, 'I'm just going into the kitchen sweetheart.' Ava glanced at him for a moment before nodding and returning her attention to Stella.

Stella mouthed the words, 'She'll be fine,' and that seemed to clinch it.

'Lead the way,' he said to Iris, who took his free hand and did so.

The kitchen was only a few feet away and the minute they stepped inside, Scott placed his glass on the counter, pulled Iris into his arms and kissed her.

She was surprised but quickly returned his kiss. It didn't last that long but Iris experienced sensations she was sure she hadn't felt before. Other than on Friday night. But his kisses then had been more restrained compared to this.

'I needed to do that,' Scott said, his eyes making it clear he would like to do a lot more.

'I'm glad you did,' she said. 'I don't know about you, but I'd quite like an early night. Unless that's too forward of me. Stella said I rush things.'

'An early night sounds perfect. But I might be the one to rush things later. It's been a long time since...' He shrugged. 'Since I've been to bed with anyone. Four years to be precise.'

Iris gasped. 'Four years! You mean ... you haven't slept with anyone since your wife died?'

He shook his head. 'I hadn't kissed anyone since then, either, until I kissed you on Friday night. Apart from Ava. But obviously that's an entirely different type of kiss. I hope ... I hope I didn't disappoint you. I'm out of practice.'

'I'd never have known. And I was the complete opposite of disappointed. But if you think you still need more practice, feel free.'

He grinned devilishly. 'I definitely need more practice. Lots and lots of it.'

He kissed her again, this time more slowly and as the kiss deepened, she thought her head might explode. His hands were in her hair and his body was pressed against hers, so much so that she could feel his heart beating and his excitement growing. And then he released her.

'Wow!' she said, gasping for breath. 'I think you actually made my toes tingle! That's never happened to me before.'

He looked her in the eye.

'You made every part of me ... tingle.' He grinned. 'You still are.' He eased her farther away. 'I think we'd better stop while we still can.'

'Must we? Yes. You're right. For now.' She blew out a breath and straightened her hair back in place. 'But can we pick up from where we left off as soon as possible, please?'

He beamed at her. 'Absolutely.'

She continued preparing dinner, which she stopped to answer the door, but she darted several looks at him and was thrilled to see his gaze was fixed intently on her.

'Need a hand?' he asked, sending ridiculous sensations coursing through her.

'Nope. What I need is a cold shower. Stop looking at me like that.'

'I can't help it. I like looking at you.'

'I like it too, but that glint in your eyes and that smile on your lips is doing things to me you wouldn't believe. Unless you want me to throw you on this counter and make mad passionate love to you right now, stop it!'

'You shouldn't have said that. Now all I'll be picturing is precisely that.' He emptied his glass, placed it on the counter and pulled her into his arms again. 'I can't believe how much I want you, Iris. I can't believe how you make me feel. I hope … I hope this isn't just a sex thing for you, like it was with Bentley, because for me, I think I'm already way past that.'

She met the look in his eyes. 'It's not just a sex thing, Scott. I've never felt like this before. Ever. Part of me is euphoric and part of me is terrified.'

'Same here. Is this crazy?'

'Yes. But it also feels so right, don't you think?'

'I do. I haven't felt like this since … since I fell in love with Veronica. Sorry. I shouldn't have mentioned her.'

'Of course you should. You loved her. She is Ava's mum. I'm a bit intimidated by the thought of her, I'll admit, but I don't want you to feel you can't mention her in front of me.' She eased herself out of his embrace. 'But I'd better get this dinner finished or Stella and Ava will come looking for us.'

'You're incredible. You do know that don't you?'

'As it happens, I do. You're pretty incredible yourself. So how did you and Veronica meet?'

He ran a hand through his hair and took in a quick breath.

'We met in a wine bar in London. I had popped in to see my mate who worked there. Veronica was meeting Trisha.' The smile slid from his face for a second. 'She was held up at work and was already late but she'd texted Veronica and asked her to wait. The minute I saw her, I knew she was going to be in my life from that moment on. I plucked up the courage to talk to her. I don't know what I said but we chatted for a while and then I asked if I could buy her a drink. By the time Trisha arrived, thirty minutes late, we were already half in love. At least I was. And Veronica always said she felt the same. We exchanged numbers. People did that in those days. Now women are understandably more careful about giving out their numbers to strange men in bars. I called her that night to see if she'd got home safely. Which was a stupid excuse, of course. But I couldn't wait. We went on our first date the very next night and we were together until ... the end.'

'How did she die?'

'Horribly. But also, quickly. She eventually faded away after being unable to bear the pain she was in. They'd given her drugs, obviously, but her cancer was aggressive and evil. And very fast. She was gone within weeks of being diagnosed. She had no idea she was ill until it was too late.'

He picked up his empty glass and Iris quickly opened another bottle of wine and refilled it, saying, 'I'm so sorry, Scott. I shouldn't have asked that.'

He shook his head. 'No. It's okay. I need to talk about it sometimes. But I think it's time to change the subject.'

'May I just ask what happened with Trisha this evening, before we do? Was it related to Veronica in any way?'

He furrowed his brows. 'To Veronica? No. Although, I suppose it was.'

'You said Trisha was worried. Did she say that she didn't think I'm the type of woman you should be with? That Veronica wouldn't have wanted you to be with me.'

He blinked a few times. 'It's as if you were there. These were her words, not mine. She said she was concerned that you don't seem capable of having a serious relationship. That all you're interested in is sex. And that Veronica would want me to be with someone who could be a good mother to Ava. I told her she didn't know anything about you and that from what I'd seen and heard so far, I thought she was wrong. But that this was a date to find those things out. The point is, I don't care about any of that when I'm with you. Somehow I know in my heart, or my intuition tells me, that this was meant to be. Just like meeting Veronica in that bar was meant to be. I didn't tell Trisha that because she was getting upset. I simply said we'd discuss it in the morning and I didn't want to talk about it in front of Ava, and I left the room.'

'She really doesn't like me, does she? I can see her point of view. She wants what's best for you and Ava. And she was Veronica's best friend, so she's protective of what she thinks her friend would've wanted. But she hasn't given me a chance. I thought it was just me, but if you say you haven't dated anyone since Veronica, maybe Stella is right. Maybe this is about you and Ava. Maybe Trisha will never think anyone is good enough for you. Or maybe she's a little afraid of losing you both if someone new comes into your life. Perhaps if you tell her that won't happen, she'll be more open. Anyone can see how much you and Ava mean to her and she means a lot to you both. Only a fool would try to end that relationship.'

He smiled slowly. 'You might be right. I assumed she knew that she'd always be a part of our lives. Perhaps I need to reassure her. But now that she's found Bentley again, maybe she'll be the one to drift away from us a little.'

'Yes. It's odd that hasn't occurred to her. That you and Ava might be worried that she'll walk away and leave you. Sorry. I think I might be making it worse. Now we should definitely change the subject. Dinner will be ready in five minutes. Why don't you go and see how Stella and Ava are getting on? And then get Stella to take you to the dining room. It's just along there.'

She pointed to the hall as he moved forward, but he stopped and kissed her briefly once more.

'You're amazing, Iris. And Veronica would've loved you.'

Chapter 21

Rosie's head was pounding. She'd already taken two headache tablets, drunk almost a litre of water and had a warm then cold shower to try to shock herself awake and out of the hangover from hell.

She had no one to blame but herself. She hadn't been running since Saturday morning and she always felt grumpy if she didn't get her exercise. The problem was it just didn't feel the same without Will beside her. But although he had asked her to run with him, she had made excuses saying that she'd already had her run, or that she wasn't feel up to it at that moment and would run later.

She didn't like lying to Will but right now she couldn't bear to be in the same room with him. If they'd been running along Clementine Cliff, which was part of their usual route, she might have been tempted to push him over the edge.

Was she being unreasonable? Stella certainly seemed to think so. She had said as much on Monday morning when Will had well and truly let the cat out of the bag about his relationship with Penny.

How could Rosie make Will see that this was a mistake? That Penny would never make a vicar's wife. He had said that it was too soon in the relationship to think that far ahead. But he clearly had. He only told her about it because it was getting serious. He'd said that on Friday when he'd stunned her with his news.

Rosie knew he was disappointed that she hadn't welcomed his revelation with open arms. That she hadn't said how wonderful it was that two people had found love. That she was happy for them and would give them her wholehearted support. But how could she say any of that when none of it was true?

She didn't welcome his news. She didn't think it was wonderful. She wasn't going to support them in any way.

And why was that?

Penny seemed pleasant enough. Odd, but nice. Did it really matter in this day and age that the woman didn't believe in God? Although she did have strange beliefs. She believed nature was sacred and that even trees were profoundly spiritual. Worse than that, rocks had hidden meanings, according to Penny Walsh. She read tarot cards and thought people should be guided by them. She had different coloured stones throughout her cottage, or so someone had told Rosie. Rosie herself had never been inside Sunnycliff Cottage. Unlike her brother, Will, who could hardly keep away these days.

Perhaps the woman had cast some spell or something over him?

Rosie laughed at that thought. That would be giving credence to Penny's ludicrous lifestyle and beliefs and there was no way Rosie would do that. Penny wasn't a witch in any event so she couldn't cast a spell. But she did come close. Or she had with Will. She had managed somehow to make the man fall in love with her. That was no mean feat. In days of old the woman would have been dragged from her cottage and burned at the stake. Such a pity some of the old ways had died out.

At least she didn't dance naked in the woods. Or if she did, no one in the village was aware of it. And someone would be. Not much happened in the village of Clementine Cove, without someone knowing about it.

Which was why it was so astonishing that Will and Penny had carried on their liaison since before the New Year and yet not one single person had mentioned it to Rosie.

And they would have. No matter how much they liked and respected her brother.

Will had begged Rosie to give Penny a chance. To be reasonable. To allow them to be happy by giving them her blessing. Or at the least, by accepting their love for one another. Rosie had said no. Stella had told her she was wrong.

And now Iris popped into Rosie's head. Wasn't Trisha doing the same to Iris? Iris was foolish and reckless and possibly addicted to sex, but she wasn't a bad person. She had proved that since moving to the village. And she had shown Stella had to use the laptop to call Marian. She hadn't needed to do that. She had even arranged for the internet to be connected to Stella's cottage. That was something Rosie had been unable to do. Trisha was wrong about Iris. Could Rosie be wrong about Penny Walsh?

The doorbell pierced Rosie's brain like an ice pick and it kept chipping away at her skull. Who would be calling at Rosehip Cottage at 8 a.m. on a Tuesday? And why wasn't Will answering it?

'All right!' Rosie shrieked, quickly wishing she hadn't as her head reverberated like a drum.

She wasn't even dressed yet but she had to stop that incessant noise. Right now she didn't care which one of Will's parishioners saw her in her dressing gown and slippers. Although she did for a brief moment wish she had put on her newest dressing gown and not the ancient one that was almost threadbare.

'What in God's name is so important that you ... Oh! It's you!'

Joe Davissen looked her up and down, raised his brows and sniggered.

How dare he?

And why did it have to be him?

Rosie looked as if she had been dragged backwards through every hedge in the garden of Rosehip Cottage and then thrown in the sea, rolled in the sand and been hung up to dry in a barrel of flour.

'Morning, love. Sorry. Rosie. I'd like to say that you are a sight for sore eyes this morning. But I'd be lying. Bad night, was it? I've come to fix your pipes. But I think I'd better get the kettle on and make you a mug of coffee. Are you going to hang your head in the hall all day or are you going to let me in?'

'Please go away. I'm not feeling well.'

'No can do, Rosie my love. I've just seen Will so I know you're here all alone. You need looking after.'

She raised her eyes to his. 'What makes you so sure I'm alone? I might have company.'

He raised his brows higher. 'P-lease. At 8 a.m. on a Tuesday? With you looking like that? Nope. I don't buy it for a second. Now step aside unless you want me to sweep you up in my arms. Which I'm more than happy to do, Rosie.'

She stepped aside as fast as she could.

'Don't even think about it,' she hissed.

He grinned. 'Too late. I've been thinking about you quite a lot. And not just how to sweep you off your feet.'

She stood at the door open-mouthed as he sauntered into the hall and then marched towards the kitchen.

'Close the door, Rosie,' he added. 'And take yourself back to bed. I'll bring you up a nice mug of coffee and a biscuit. That'll do you the world of good.'

She considered arguing with him but she had neither the strength nor the will power, and somehow, she thought he might win. But as she trudged up the stairs to her room, she couldn't quite believe that a plumber was telling her what to do and more astonishingly, she was doing as he told her.

She clambered back into her bed and pulled the covers up around her chin.

It was only when Joe appeared with a steaming mug of coffee and a plate of chocolate digestives that she realised she had left her computer switched on, and that she was still logged in to at least three of the online interactive live casinos.

Naturally, because the man seemed to have a sixth sense, he spotted her computer screen was on immediately he entered the room. He placed the mug and plate on her bedside table and walked towards her desk.

'I like your screensaver,' he said, smiling at the sleek and gleaming, sleeping leopard. 'But I'm turning this off because you clearly need to get some sleep.'

'I'll do it in a moment,' she said. 'I'm still logged in to some sites and I need to log out.'

'I can do that for you,' he said. 'Unless there's something you don't want me to see. Are you on some dating sites, or something?'

He was grinning when he turned to look at her but once he'd looked back and seen the three open windows of the casinos appear in place of the screensaver, his smile disappeared and when he turned to her again, his face was serious.

'Not what I was expecting,' he said. 'How long have you been gambling online?'

'It is really none of your business. You shouldn't be near my computer. You shouldn't be in my room. And don't you dare judge me.'

'Are you an addict?'

'No!'

'And yet you've got three separate sites running at once?'

'I ... I ... It's none of your business!'

'Shouting at me won't help you. Does Will know about this?'

She sat upright and screamed at him. 'No! And don't you dare tell him!'

'Screaming at me will help you even less. How large are your losses?'

She gasped. 'What makes you think I'm in the red? I bought this watch with my winnings I'll have you know.'

'Lucky you. But everyone who gambles ends up losing, Rosie. And this explains the way you look this morning.'

He had spotted the two empty bottles of red wine and he shook his head when he looked at her.

'So I had a few glasses of wine. It's not a crime.'

'It's not. But it is a waste of your time and money to get as drunk as you clearly did and then, no doubt, lose even more money on these sites. It's your life, Rosie and I'm not your brother. I'm not even a friend in your eyes. But I like you so I'm going to say this. Gambling and drinking are addictive. They're also often a cry for help. I have no idea how long you've been on this path but if you would like to get off it, I'd like to help. There are better ways to spend your time. And better ways to get excitement.'

'I'm not an addict. I'm honestly not. I can stop whenever I like.'

'Then stop. Stop today. If only to prove to me that you can. I'm going to log you out of these, Rosie and I hope you find the strength not to log back in. This is not the wisest way to spend your money or your time.'

'It's just a bit of fun and excitement,' she said, suddenly feeling ashamed. 'I always kept within my limits until ... until I got some bad news on Friday. Since then I've felt ... lost. But why am I telling you this? If you tell anyone about this, I'll ... Oh. You won't, will you?'

'No, Rosie. I won't. I won't even tell your brother. But I think you should. And I think you should talk to your friends. I believe you. I don't think you're addicted. Yet. But if you don't stop this now, you soon might be. Here's something for you to think about. Instead of gambling and drinking to excess, why don't you go really mad and come out on a date with me? I'll take you for a ride on the back of my Harley and give you the thrill of your life.' He smiled at her and one by one, logged her out of the casinos.

'You want to take me out? On a date? After seeing me like this?'

He nodded. 'I think I've seen you at your worst. So we've got that over with.'

'I don't date people like … I'm sorry. What I meant to say is that I don't date people I hardly know.'

'Especially one of The Great Unwashed. Yes. I know about that. Nothing remains a secret in this village for ever. You're a snob, Rosie. But I like you. And I think you could like me. If you let yourself get over the fact that I'm a plumber, and in your opinion, several rungs of the ladder beneath you.'

She had gasped at that. 'Then why on Earth do you want to date me?'

'Because I think, deep down. Very, very deep down, there's a nice woman struggling to get out. And because we don't choose who we fall in love with, do we? Just ask Will. Now I'm not saying I'm in love with you, so hold your horses. What I'm saying is I've liked you from a distance for a long, long time. And now I've had a chance to talk to you and exchange some banter, I like you a little bit more. Why don't we see if this could grow into something we might both enjoy? You're not perfect and neither am I. I'll leave you to think about it. I'll be downstairs fixing the pipes if you want to chat some more. Now drink your coffee, eat your biscuits and get some sleep. Pleasant dreams.'

For once in her life, Rosie couldn't think of anything to say.

Chapter 22

'I hear you're buying lunch,' Elodie said, sitting on the seat opposite Iris at their favourite table in the window of Cove Café Bistro.

'Brunch. My text said brunch. Stella will be joining us. And possibly Rosie. Although Stella says she called her, and Rosie's not feeling well, so we'll see. Aren't you going to ask me about last night?'

'Give me a chance! I've only just sat down. I wondered why your text said to meet at 11.30, which is far too early for lunch. And I don't have a lot of time this morning, sadly. But anyway. I don't have to ask, because for one thing you're dying to tell me and for another, there's a smile on your face the size of China. Went well, did it?'

Iris flopped forward spreading her arms out across the table towards Elodie and then slapping her hands against the surface as if she were playing bongo drums.

'Went well! That's the understatement of the century.' She pulled herself upright. 'Although it did get off to a slightly rocky start. You'll never believe this. He was late because Trisha had words with him! About me! I'm beginning to think she may be a bit of a cow.'

'What do you mean, "had words with him"? What did she say? Oh, hi Harley. May I just have a coffee for now, please? I think we're waiting for others.'

'Good morning, Elodie.' Harley smiled, took one of the cups from the tray she was carrying, and placed a steaming cup of milky coffee in front of Elodie.

Elodie gave a little gasp and laughed, looking from the cup to Iris and then to Harley.

'This is exactly how I like it! You're a star, Harley.'

'Thanks. But Iris told me you'd be joining her and that you'd want a coffee, so I can't take the credit. Enjoy.'

Iris grinned. 'Take the credit, Harley.'

Harley grinned back and went off to deliver the other beverages on her tray.

'Where were we?' Elodie said, glancing at Iris over the rim of her cup.

'Trisha,' Iris said, frowning. 'She told him she's concerned that I don't seem capable of having a serious relationship. That all I'm interested in is sex. And that Veronica would want him to be with someone who could be a good mother to Ava.'

'Oh my God! She is a cow. How does she know whether you'd be a good mother or not? But she's not wrong about the sex bit, is she?'

'No. I'll give her that. But it's only because I hadn't met the right man. Until now. Now everything's changed. And yes, we only met a few days ago, but this feels so different from anything I've experienced before. Last night was ... I know it's corny to say it was the best sex I've ever had – but it was! It really was. Even the cuddling was better. And we talked and talked. And laughed. Oh I don't know. I can't really explain it. It felt as if Scott and I were the only people on the planet. And when I think about him – like I was before you arrived – I'm not just thinking about how great the sex is. I'm actually thinking about *him*. In fact, I can't seem to stop thinking about him. His smile. His laugh. His voice. Even the way he is with Ava. And that's another thing. I never thought I'd hear myself say this, but I really like Ava. A five-year-old kid! Can you believe that? I enjoyed spending time with her last night. We all played games. We talked about things she likes. She got so excited when the fox was playing in the garden. I told her I see him almost every day and she asked if she could live with me! Well, live in the cottage so that she could see the fox every day, but still. And suddenly, I'm imagining how wonderful it would be if she did. Live with me I mean. And Scott, obviously.'

'Obviously. Wow! You're serious, aren't you? You really do want this. Iris Talbot. I think you've finally grown up. And I'm pretty certain, Scott Fitzgerald is The One. Hmm. Iris Fitzgerald. That's got a nice ring to it.'

Iris flopped against the back of her seat. 'It has, hasn't it? Oh, El. I really hope he is. Because as crazy as this sounds, I don't think my life could ever be as good without him and Ava in it.'

'Then we just need to get Trisha to stop being a cow, don't we?'

Iris snorted derisively. 'Good luck with that. I don't think she'll ever like me. But maybe it's not just me. She'll never think anyone is good enough for Scott and Ava. Or maybe she is afraid of losing them if someone new comes into his life. I told Scott that, last night. He's going to tell her that she'll always be a part of our lives. If things do go the way we hope they will with us.'

Elodie beamed at her. 'So he's feeling the same as you? Oh, Iris! That's fantastic! I'm so, so happy for you.'

'Me too.' Iris took a sip of her coffee and then sighed softly and smiled broadly. 'So this is what True Love feels like? It's pretty great, isn't it? Who knew?'

'Still smiling, I see.' Stella approached the table and Elodie moved over one seat.

'I'll be smiling for the rest of my life. Thanks to you.'

'Me?' Stella nodded a greeting to Elodie. 'I don't think I'm the one who put that smile on your face, Iris.'

'No. But it wouldn't be there if you hadn't stepped in and saved the day. Well, night. If you hadn't been there to look after Ava.'

Stella gently tapped Iris on the hand. 'It was my pleasure. I can't remember the last time I had such fun. It took me back, I can tell you.' She let out a wistful sigh. 'I hadn't realised how much I miss it. Being with young, lively minds. I think I need to get out more.' She grinned at Iris and Elodie. 'Although ... now you've shown me all the wonders of the internet, going out more might be the last thing I want to do once my connection is up and running at home.' She laughed.

'Don't become one of those people who spend their days in front of a computer screen,' Elodie said. 'Use it to find out where the action is and go out there and get it.'

Stella laughed louder. 'You're forgetting I'm seventy-five, my dear. Not in my thirties like the two of you.'

'You're never too old to have fun,' Iris said. 'And seventy-five is the new fifty-five. Oh. Speaking of which. Here's Rosie.' Iris nodded towards the door as Rosie staggered in the direction of the table.

Elodie glanced around and then met Iris' eye. 'She doesn't look well at all.'

Iris moved over. 'Sit down before you fall down, Rosie.'

'Should you be out?' Stella asked.

'I had to.' Rosie flopped onto the seat Iris had vacated, and groaned. 'Don't worry. It's not contagious. I merely had one glass of wine too many last night, and then I didn't get a wink of sleep.'

'Then shouldn't you have stayed in bed?' Elodie said.

'I couldn't. That damn man kept fussing over me. I had to get out of the house.'

'Will?' Stella seemed surprised.

'No. Joe. Could someone kindly order me a coffee, please? Large. Black. Make it two.'

'Who's Joe?' Iris grinned. 'Got yourself a man, have you Rosie?'

'Good heavens!' Stella said. 'You're blushing. Or are you having a hot flush?'

'Isn't Joe the name of Harley's dad?' Elodie queried, waving at Harley to get her attention.

'Oh Rosie!' Iris said. 'Don't tell us you're having a fling with a plumber.' She roared with laughter.

'Would you all please stop shouting! And laughing.' Rosie glowered at Iris. 'I am not having a fling. Or a hot flush. And I am not blushing. It's hot in here, that's all.'

'Harley?' Elodie said, as Harley came towards them. 'Rosie needs a very large, strong, black coffee, please.'

'Coming right up.'

'Then why was the man fussing over you?' Iris asked, still grinning.

'Because ... because he came to do some work and when I answered the door, he could see I wasn't ... feeling my best. He insisted I get some sleep, and that I drink and eat and ... Oh all sorts of other things. He behaved as though he owned the place. I had to creep out without him seeing. From my own house. While he was in the cellar.' She shook her head and groaned again.

Iris exchanged glances with Elodie and Stella.

'Don't you think you should have told him you were going out?' Stella asked.

'I'm surprised you would leave someone in your house, alone,' Elodie said. 'Or is your brother there?'

Rosie's head shot up. 'No. Will's ... I don't know where Will is. Though I think I could hazard a guess.'

'The church?' Iris said.

'Penny's,' said Stella.

'Penny?' queried Elodie.

'Penny Walsh,' replied Stella. 'Hermione Dunmore's sister.'

'Oh yes.' Elodie smiled. 'I saw them here together yesterday.'

'Everyone did,' Rosie said. 'And Will's not bothered in the slightest.'

'Should he be?' Iris looked at Stella.

'Of course not,' Stella said, emphatically. 'Rosie is being unreasonable.'

'Aren't you pleased for him?' Elodie said. 'I don't know what's going on with them but he was holding her hand yesterday, so I assume they're a couple.'

'He's been seeing her since shortly after Stanley's funeral,' Rosie said. 'Without my knowledge or consent, I might add.'

'Does he need your permission?' Iris said.

'That's not what I meant. I'm simply astonished he didn't tell me. Especially as it's Penny Walsh.'

'What's wrong with Penny Walsh?' Iris asked. 'You know, people really shouldn't be so judgmental. Just because a person doesn't behave in the way you would, it doesn't make them a bad person.'

'I didn't say she was a bad person, exactly.'

Elodie tutted. 'I think Iris was referring to people in general, Rosie. And to another situation. But what is wrong with Penny? She seems really nice. She's always friendly.'

'Oh I know. Ah. Thank you, Harley.'

Harley slid the large black coffee in front of Rosie and hovered nervously beside the table.

'What's wrong, Harley?' Elodie said.

'Er. I'm not sure. Dad's just phoned to ask if Rosie's here.' She looked worried. 'I don't know what's going on but he sounded concerned and I didn't want to lie to my dad, so I said she was. I hope that's okay, Rosie.'

Everyone looked at Rosie and to Iris' surprise, she smiled.

'It's fine, Harley. What did he say when you said yes?'

'Er. He said, "Thank God for that. I was worried. Tell her I'll be here when she gets back." And then he asked how my day was going.' She shook her head as if she were utterly bemused.

'And how is your day going?' Rosie asked, still smiling.

'Really well, thanks.' Harley sounded relieved. 'Is there anything else I can get you?'

'Not for me, thank you. Does anyone else want anything?' Rosie glanced around the table. 'Why do you all look as if you've seen the Angel Gabriel, or something?'

Iris sniggered. 'Because we've all just witnessed a miracle.'

'What miracle?'

Stella laughed. 'You being nice, Rosie, and asking if we wanted anything.'

Rosie tutted, but the smile was quickly back in place.

Elodie's phone pinged and she glanced at the screen. 'Sorry, everyone, but I've got to go. Archer's parents have arrived. I'll see you all later.'

Harley moved aside and Stella got up to let Elodie out as they all said goodbye to Elodie.

'I'm starving,' Iris said. 'Let's have something to eat. I'll have the Marian's Mega Breakfast, please.'

'And for me, please,' said Stella, as she sat back down.

'I'll have the same, please,' Rosie said.

'Okay, Rosie,' Iris said, the moment Harley was out of earshot. 'Spill. And don't tell us there's nothing going on. The man was worried about you.'

Rosie's smile was unbelievable, and she blushed from ear to ear. 'Nothing's happened. I assure you. But ... it might. I don't know. He's at least five years younger, I think. And I don't need to tell either of you that he's definitely not the type of person I would usually consider dating. I really don't understand it at all. I seem to be ... attracted to him. And yet it's more than that. He's irritating. His sense of humour leaves a lot to be desired. He owns a motorbike. He's ... a plumber.' She smiled. 'It's ridiculous. It really is. I actually don't care. I truly don't! Isn't that amazing? He makes me feel ... as if the sun has come out after years and years of cloudy days.'

'Crikey, Rosie!' Iris said. 'Er. Then why did you need to get out of the house?'

Rosie blushed even more. 'Because he asked me to go out on a date, and he told me to think about it. If I hadn't come here, I might've said yes.'

'Okay. Now I'm completely confused.' Iris looked her in the eye. 'You like him and he likes you. He's asked you out and you want to go. Am I being blind here? Only I really don't see the problem.'

'Rosie is the problem,' Stella said.

Rosie nodded. 'Precisely.'

'What? Someone needs to explain.' Iris shook her head.

'You know what Rosie's like.' Stella smiled at Rosie. 'I mean no offence here, but I know you'll agree. You do have some very odd ways of seeing people in terms of their status, rather than their personality, and judging them without giving them a chance.'

'I do.' Rosie nodded. 'Like Penny, for example.'

'Yes. Like Penny. She makes Will happy. He accepts and loves her for who and what she is. You should do that too. And now you've discovered that you're attracted to a man that you never, even for a second, thought would appeal to you in any way. And rather than admit you might have been wrong about certain things your whole life, and accept those feelings, you run away.'

Rosie nodded. 'It's true. I've done nothing other than turn this all over and over in my head for the last few hours. I need to give the man a chance. I need to give myself a chance. Nothing else has made me happy. Perhaps I should take a leaf out of Will's book and try something new. Even if it's something that terrifies me. Something I would never have considered possible.'

'Wow, Rosie.' Iris stared at her. 'I never expected to hear you say anything like that.'

Rosie laughed. 'I never expected it either. I think I may be in a state of shock. Or perhaps this is my wake up call. I've been drifting through my life rather than living it. I thought I was content. I'm not. I thought I was happy. The truth is, I'm not sure what it means to be genuinely happy. I've seen Will change over the last few days since he came out into the open about his relationship with Penny. I've tried to ignore it but I can't. Will is happy. The only fly in his ointment now is me. I need to tell Will I want him to be happy. I must learn to accept Penny for the person she is, not the person I think she should be. I need to change. I'm not sure if I can, but I must try, mustn't I?'

'Yes,' said Stella. 'You must. I'm delighted you've finally met someone who has made you see that is possible.'

'Does this mean you're going to say yes to Joe?' Iris asked.

Rosie smiled. 'Yes. I think it does. But the idea frightens the life out of me. And it's been years since I've been out on a date.'

'You could invite Joe, and Penny, for dinner,' Iris suggested. 'I did that with Scott and Ava last night and it was wonderful. That would show Will and Penny that you're happy about their relationship, plus, it would mean you don't have to be entirely on your own with Joe right away.'

'That's a very good idea,' Stella said.

'It's an excellent idea,' said Rosie. 'I don't know why I didn't think of that myself.'

Chapter 23

Thursday came round far too quickly for Iris. Not only was it the day the restaurant in Cove Café Bistro was opening, it was Elodie's last day in Clementine Cove. She and Archer were leaving on Friday and would be gone for at least three months.

Iris was happy for them, but she still wasn't sure how she would feel not be able to see her best friend every day.

'You miss Marian a lot, don't you?' she asked Stella that morning in the café.

Stella nodded. 'Yes. Not as much since you've shown me how to make those video calls, and I'll be forever in your debt for that, but even so, it's not quite the same thing as having her here in the flesh. I can't hug her. I can't squeeze her hand. Silly, I know. But seeing how happy she is, helps a great deal. I'd rather see her happy miles away from me than miserable here in the village. You're wondering how you'll feel when Elodie leaves, aren't you?'

'Yep. I can't imagine it. It feels as if I'm losing an arm or something. I know she's coming back, but it still frightens me. What if they decide to stay out there? What if Archer doesn't want to leave his daughter? What if something happens?'

'Now, now.' Stella tapped her hand. 'Nothing is likely to happen. Yes, it is a possibility. No one knows what life has in store. But it is unlikely. As for them staying there, perhaps. But again, it's unlikely. Archer has the pub, and this place now. Elodie has repeatedly said she wouldn't want to live in Australia. I've heard that myself. And I don't think Archer would either. His daughter can come here to visit and he can go out there. Money isn't an issue for them, so all they need to do is hop on a plane. Besides, you may have your own decisions to make about where to live. Perhaps you'll be the one to leave Clementine Cove.'

'What? Why would I leave here? I love it here.'

Stella raised her brows. 'Scott lives in London, doesn't he? If things work out the way we both think they will, you might want to move to be with him and Ava.'

'Move back to London? I hadn't thought about that. How stupid of me. You see! It's this sort of thing I'll need to discuss with El. Except she'll be thousands of miles away and in a different time zone.'

'But you will still be able to discuss it with her. And I know we are poor substitutes, but myself and Rosie will be here for you, should you need us.'

'Thanks, Stella. That means a lot. It's weird, isn't it? There's about twenty years between me and Rosie, and forty years between you and me, and yet recently it feels as if we're all about the same age, doesn't it? Or is it just me who feels that?'

Stella laughed. 'No. I was saying the same thing to Rosie at choir practice last night. Did you know that she's finally done it? No of course you don't. She only did it last night before she came to church. She's invited Penny and Joe to dinner. It's tomorrow night.'

'Really? That's great. Part of me thought she just said all that due to lack of sleep and being hungover. I expected her to revert back to the same old Rosie as soon as she recovered. Good for her. I bet Will was surprised.'

'He was. I wasn't there when she said it but he came to choir practice looking as if a great weight had been lifted from his shoulders. She told me that he couldn't quite believe it when she made the suggestion. He was so surprised he asked her twice whether she was sure.'

'And Joe? How did he take it?'

Stella laughed. 'Apparently, he told Rosie that she won't regret it. And Rosie told him that she was already. I met him briefly and I have to say, I think he'll be good for her.'

'I wonder what Harley thinks about it.'

'She's thrilled, according to Rosie. It seems Joe has admired Rosie from afar for many years. Can you believe that? He even knew that she thought of him as one of The Great Unwashed, and that didn't put him off. But he couldn't summon up the courage to ask her out, because he knew she would shoot him down without as much as a second thought.'

'So if Rosie hadn't needed a plumber, and Harley hadn't suggested her dad, they would never have gone out together? Wow!'

'I think Joe might eventually have found a way to meet her. He said he considered joining the choir but that his singing voice makes a dog with a sore throat sound more melodious, so he thought it wouldn't help his cause.'

'I really like the sound of him. I can't wait to meet him. It's weird, isn't it, that after all this time, both Will and Rosie meet people within months of one another?'

'I suppose it is. Life works in mysterious ways.'

'Do you think Penny will move into the rectory if she and Will get married? And if so, will Rosie move out? Perhaps she could move into Penny's cottage. Or maybe she'll move in with Joe.' Iris laughed. 'On the new estate! Can you imagine that?'

'No,' said Stella, laughing. 'That I definitely can't imagine. Don't mention that to Rosie or she'll call the whole thing off right now.'

'I won't. Seriously though. If they do fall in love and stay together, they'll have to live somewhere, won't they?'

'Perhaps they'll buy somewhere else. But I think we may be getting ahead of ourselves. They haven't been on their date yet.'

Iris looked at Stella. 'What about you, Stella? Everyone seems to be falling in love, or going on dates. Wouldn't you like to meet someone special?'

Stella looked as if she'd been caught with her hand in the biscuit tin.

'Me? No. I'm far too old for all that.'

'No you're not. You're seventy-five. You could live for another twenty years or more. You were in love once, weren't you? I know you were so there's no point in denying it. What happened?'

'Good morning!'

Rosie hurried to join them. Iris hadn't seen her come in.

'You're looking a lot better than you did the last time I saw you.'

'I'm feeling much better, thank you. How are you, Iris? And how are things going with Scott?' She sat on the chair beside Stella and waved at Harley.

'I'm good, thanks. Things are going well, but Trisha is still being a pain. He couldn't stay on Tuesday night because Trisha said it wasn't right for Ava to know he was spending the night away from her. And I was going to stay at The Lighthouse last night but she made things so awkward that I finally decided to just go home. Luckily for us, Stella has offered to come and stay at my place again tonight so Scott and I are coming here for dinner.'

'That Trisha sounds as awful as I used to be. Don't let her win.'

'I don't intend to.'

'Hi Rosie,' Harley said, beaming at her. 'Dad is so excited about Friday. He won't stop talking about it. Oh sorry. Is this weird? I shouldn't talk about it at work, should I? What can I get you?'

'I don't mind at all,' Rosie said. 'And I know Stella and Iris don't. Between you and I, Harley, I'm excited too. I'd love a black coffee please. And a slice of coffee and walnut cake. Do you ladies want anything?'

'We're good, thanks,' Iris said.

'Have I missed anything?' Rosie asked, once Harley had gone. 'What were you two talking about when I arrived?'

'Nothing,' Stella said.

'I was saying how everyone seems to be finding someone special and asking Stella if she'd like someone too. And also, trying to find out about her past. I think there's–'

'I'm far too old,' Stella interrupted, sharply.

'No you're not,' Iris repeated.

'A few weeks ago I would've agreed with you, Stella, but now I agree with Iris. We need to live our lives to the full. Have you ever been in love, Stella? I don't think I've ever asked.'

'No, you haven't.'

'Well have you?'

'I'd really rather not discuss things that happened a lifetime ago. I think it's wonderful that so many people are finding love, but it's not something I'm looking for at this stage in my life.'

'What about friendship and companionship?' Iris said. 'You could have that.'

'I've got that. With you two and with everyone in the village, and with Marian, of course, when she returns.'

'We won't keep you warm at night,' Rosie said.

'I've got a hot water bottle for that,' said Stella. 'Besides, the nights are warmer now, and we've got the summer to look forward to.'

'I think we should set you up on a dating site,' said Rosie. 'Now that you're getting on board the technology train.'

'You'll do no such thing!'

'Okay,' Iris said. 'Maybe not a dating site. But what about finding people with shared interests?'

'I'm happy as I am, but thank you for the thought.'

'I thought I was happy,' Rosie said. 'I was wrong.'

'I'm not you, Rosie.'

'I'm well aware of that. But you are lonely sometimes, aren't you?'

Stella looked anxious. 'We all get lonely sometimes. Even those who are surrounded by people can feel lonely. But it soon passes.'

'So does time,' Rosie said. 'And you're not getting any younger.'

'Was there really no one that you've ever loved?' Iris persisted. 'I'm sure there was.

Why don't you want to talk about it? Did it end badly? Just tell me that and I'll shut up.'

Stella puffed out a sigh. 'Oh for Heaven's sake, Iris. All right. Yes. There was someone once. A lifetime ago. And yes, it ended badly.'

'There was?' Rosie screeched. 'How did I not know this? Did Stanley Talbot know? Did he have a file on you, Stella?'

'Stanley didn't know. He thought he knew everything, but he didn't. And the reason you don't know about it is because no one does. Now let's change the subject.'

'Not so fast,' said Rosie. 'I need details. Iris promised to shut up but I didn't.'

Stella glared at her. 'There is no point in discussing it. It was fifty years ago, Rosamunde. It's over and forgotten.'

'It's clearly not forgotten. You wouldn't be getting cross if it was forgotten. Why won't you tell us? Iris tells us everything. Far more than we want to know, sometimes. And I opened my heart and soul to you both on Tuesday. If it was so long ago, what harm can it do to talk about it now?'

'Perhaps it's still painful,' Iris said. 'I'm sorry Stella.'

'Pain shared is pain halved. But how could it still be painful after so long? Unless he was the great love of your life. The only man you've ever loved. Oh my goodness. Was he?'

Harley came back with the coffee and cake as Stella glowered at Rosie.

'Yes. You want to know? All right. I'll tell you. But don't you dare judge me, Rosie.'

'Judge you? Why would I judge you for being in love?'

'Because Yves was married. That's why.'

Rosie blinked several times, as did Iris.

'Married?' Iris said. 'I'm not judging, Stella. Honestly I'm not. But you're the last person I would ever expect to have an affair.'

'Same here,' Rosie said. 'What a dark horse you are, Stella!'

'Not that it's a big deal,' Iris added. 'It happens all the time and no one bats an eye.'

'Not now,' Stella said. 'But fifty years ago, most people still did. And it was fifty-five years ago, to be precise.'

'And his name was Yves?' Iris said. 'I like that. Was he French?'

'Wait!' said Rosie. 'Yves? Or Eve? Was it a woman? Is that why you've never spoken of it? Not that it matters.'

'Yves was a man, Rosie. And the reason I've never spoken of it is because he was married and I was ashamed. I was made to feel ashamed. By my parents, by his family. Obviously by his wife. By anyone who knew. When I returned home here, my mother said I must never speak of it again. And I haven't. Until now.'

'Wow.' Iris shook her head. 'How awful. I can't imagine keeping that a secret for my entire life.'

'That's because you never keep anything secret,' Rosie said.

Iris shrugged. 'That's true. I'm an open book.'

'So,' said Rosie, nudging Stella's arm. 'The secret's out now so you may as well tell us all about it.'

Stella hesitated for a moment or two and then her expression changed and it was as though she were somewhere far off, at least in her mind.

'Yves' family owned a lot of land in the hills above Menton in the South of France. Lemons were once a major part of the local economy and Menton was one of the main lemon producers in Europe. When tourists began to arrive, many people happily sold off their land to wealthy foreigners, and holiday villas replaced lemon groves. But Yves' family held on to theirs and they married into other land-owning families. Instead of just growing lemons, his extended family also grew olives and lavender. Needless to say, they were rich. I was taking a year out before I went to university. Not many people did that then but my parents were both teachers and they believed travel expanded the mind. A friend of my mother's was married to a member of Yves' family. An uncle. They suggested I could go and stay with them and help out with all the harvests.'

'That sounds like fun,' Iris said, when Stella paused. 'But also hard work, I suspect.'

'It was. I arrived in mid-September. Olives are harvested from late September right through until November or even, as in the case of these olives, into December. I can still smell those olives being pressed into the richest, darkest, deepest yellowy-green olive oil. I met Yves on my very first day. I think we both knew then that something would happen between us, although at the time, Yves was engaged. But he wasn't married. We spent months trying to avoid one another and yet at the same time, we couldn't keep away from each other. So many times we came close, but something always stopped us.' She shook her head and sighed.

'Nothing like sexual tension to make the heart soar,' said Rosie.

'You could cut the tension with a knife,' said Stella. 'It was as though electricity filled the air when we were near to one another. Harvesting the lemons began in mid-December and continued until April. The lemons are picked as they become ripe, so we had to visit the trees on a daily basis. We shared our first kiss on Christmas Eve beneath a sprig of mistletoe that my mother's friend had hung above her kitchen door. No one saw us because we knew that it was wrong, but we couldn't hold off any longer.' She touched her fingers to her lips. 'I can still remember that kiss. Still feel it on my lips, even after all these years. That first kiss of so many and yet that's the one I recall the most vividly.'

'It's often the way,' said Iris. 'Or so I've heard. Sorry. What happened then?'

'Yves got married.'

'No! What? Why?'

'Because he was engaged and it was all arranged. His family wanted it. Her family wanted it. Everyone wanted it. Apart from me. And Yves. But he couldn't and wouldn't go against his family and he wouldn't embarrass them by breaking off the engagement for something that might not have lasted; a relationship his family would never accept nor agree to. To be with me at that time would've meant Yves leaving his family and everything he knew and loved. I couldn't ask him to do that. And he agreed we should try to stay away from one another. Which we did. For a while. Even though my heart was breaking.'

'But it didn't end there?' Iris asked.

'No. In Menton, each February, there's a festival called the Fête du Citron. It's famous for its impressive sculptures made from hundreds of tonnes of citrus fruits. But the fruits are brought in from Spain, due to a shortage of local produce. It was during that festival that Yves and I made love for the first time. After our kiss on Christmas Eve, we'd kissed a couple of times, but nothing more. When he got married in January, that stopped. After that festival, there was no stopping us. I was head over heels in love. I'd already given him my heart. Now I gave him my body, willingly and wantonly. I gave myself completely to a man who loved me as deeply as I loved him, but to a man I could never have. We met in secret as often as we could. By the spring, Yves was talking of leaving his wife. Of losing everything to be with me. And then he discovered she was pregnant.'

'So he was still sleeping with her, even though he said he loved you!' Iris was furious.

'No. He said he wasn't and I believed him. But he had been, until the festival in February. She was already pregnant by then, but we had no idea. He didn't know. He told me as soon as he did. But we still couldn't keep our hands off each other. During the lavender harvest in mid-July, we were like rabbits. Those long, hot days and sultry nights, our bodies, sweaty and tired from intensive labour, but still eager to make passionate love will stay with me till the day I die. But by the end of that harvest, in August, the truth had all come out. The fact that Yves was no longer behaving like a husband to his wife. That I was the one he spent every moment he could with. There was a huge scene, as you can no doubt imagine, and his family told him it had to end. And then his wife was rushed into hospital that same day and his son was born early but both his wife and child nearly died. His family said it was because of what he'd done. What we'd done. I was sent packing, obviously, and Yves made his choice. He chose to stay with his wife and son. Although, to be fair to him, he did say that if I asked him to, he would leave to be with me. I couldn't do that, could I? He would hate me, eventually. I know I would've hated myself. Except, sometimes, I wish I had asked him to.' She shrugged. 'It took me a long time to get over it. In truth, I never really have. I still love him, even now. But I came home and faced the music and went to uni, got my degree and became a teacher. And the woman I am now. And now you know it all.'

Chapter 24

The opening of the restaurant in Cove Café Bistro was a complete success, just as the reopening of the café had been. The restaurant was fully booked even though the food and drink at this event was not free. But the prices were discounted.

Iris was still thinking about the love story Stella had told her and Rosie. Both of them had been astonished. It was so strange that you could know someone and yet have no idea what had happened to them during their lives.

Stella had said that Iris could tell Scott, and even Elodie and she had. Mainly because Stella knew her well enough to know that Iris found it difficult to keep secrets from her friends and those she cared about. Even other people's secrets.

Scott and Elodie had been as surprised as Iris had been, but it was Elodie who suggested that Iris should look Yves up and see if he was still around and, more importantly, still with wife.

'Wouldn't it be romantic if he were now free? He and Stella could get in touch. They could meet up. They could fall in love all over again.'

Iris laughed. 'You've been watching too many romance films.'

But the seed was sown in her mind and when she mentioned it to Scott over dinner after she'd told him the story, he seemed to think it was a nice idea.

'So you would be pleased if an old lover of yours got in touch after fifty-five years?'

'I suppose it would depend on who the old lover was, but if I were in Yves' shoes, yes, I think so. It's difficult to know because we aren't sure what happened with his wife. If she's still around, she might not be happy and that might stir up old wounds.'

'True. Why would it depend on who the old lover was? For you I mean. Are there a lot?'

He grinned. 'Are you jealous?'

'No. Maybe. It depends.'

He laughed at that and took her hand in his across the table and kissed her fingers.

'There's no need to be. Other than Veronica and you, I don't have any old lovers. Or young lovers.'

'What? Are you telling me that you've only slept with Veronica and now me?'

'Yes. I've lived a sheltered life, obviously. Does that bother you? You look worried. Is something wrong?'

'No. Nothing. But perhaps this helps explain why Trisha dislikes me so much. If she knows you've only slept with two women.'

'I don't tell Trisha how many women I have or haven't slept with.'

'Okay. Er. I'm not sure if I should tell you this, bearing in mind what you've just told me, but you and Bentley aren't the only guys I've slept with. Please don't hate me and please say it doesn't matter.'

He tightened his hold on her fingers, giving them a reassuring squeeze.

'I could never hate you, Iris. And no, it doesn't matter. But if it's all the same with you, I'd honestly rather not know how many there have been. Not because I would think less of you if the number is huge. I wouldn't. But because I might start to get anxiety over having to compete with a lot of previous lovers.'

'Believe me, Scott, there is no competition. You outshone all of them the very first time we made love. And if anything, it's only got better since then.'

He grinned. 'Since Monday night? Bearing in mind it's only Thursday today.'

'Ye-s. But we have made love a lot in that time.'

'We have, haven't we? But not as much as I'd like. Shall we skip dessert?'

'We'll get it to take away. We might feel hungry later.'

Chapter 25

The following day, when she and Stella and Rosie all met up again in Cove Café Bistro, Iris was determined to mention the idea of getting in touch with Yves.

'Have Elodie and Archer left?' Stella asked the minute she arrived.

Iris was sitting at the usual table and she nodded. 'Yep. We had breakfast together this morning. I cried. Actually we both did. But I'm okay now. I don't think it's really sunk in yet that I won't be seeing her in here, or the pub, or anywhere in Clementine Cove for several months.'

'You'll be fine. And the time will fly.'

Rosie joined them a moment later.

'They've gone then? Are you okay?'

'Yep. I'll be fine, thanks. But I don't want to talk about it, if you don't mind, because I might get all emotional again.'

'I don't mind. I saw that Trisha woman last night at the opening. You're right. She definitely hates you. If looks could kill you wouldn't be sitting here right now.'

'What? I saw her briefly but only for a moment. Mind you, I was so wrapped up in Scott that I didn't really notice anyone else. I didn't even see you, Rosie. You should've come and said hello.'

'No. You were all loved up and I didn't want to interrupt.'

'That's very unlike you,' Stella said.

'What can I say? I'm a changed woman? I noticed something else though. I know Bentley and Trisha are supposed to be rekindling their romance, but Trisha spent the entire time I saw her, staring at you and Scott. And Bentley spent most of his time chatting and laughing with everyone else, but in particular, with Nina.'

'Nina? Harley's aunt?' asked Iris.

'The very same. I like her. And as she's Joe's sister, I suppose that's good.'

'They do seem to get on well,' Iris said. 'Nina and Bentley, I mean. Not Joe and his sister. Although I'm sure they do too.'

'Yes,' said Stella. 'Even I've noticed that. Nina's working here part time, but on a permanent basis now. Did you know that?'

'Yes. Elodie and Archer told me the other day. This place has been so busy since the reopening and with the restaurant too, they decided to employ more staff. I'm glad that she and Bentley are becoming friends. I think, if he stays with Trisha, he might need all the friends he can get.'

Stella smiled. 'Friendships are certainly blossoming in Clementine Cove. There's Will and Penny. Although that's in full bloom. There's Rosie and Joe. That's in bud. There's you and Scott. That's virtually a bouquet. And there's Bentley and Nina.'

'You mean Bentley and Trisha,' Rosie corrected.

'No. I mean Bentley and Nina. I think we may see some surprises before too long.'

'Speaking of friends and surprises, Stella, would you be really cross if I told you that a certain lemon, olive and lavender farm in the hills of Menton is on the internet and I happened to look it up?'

'What?' Stella went deathly pale and her hands flew to her chest.

'She's having a heart attack!' Rosie shrieked.

'Oh God! I'll phone an ambulance!'

'You'll do no such thing, Iris!' Stella took several deep breaths. 'And I am not having a heart attack. It was merely a shock. A severe shock. But I'm fine. Are you telling me that you looked up Yves' family?'

'No. I looked up Yves. And he's still alive and running the farm with his son. No mention of a wife.'

They all exchanged glances.

'Maybe she's left him?' Rosie suggested. 'Or she's dead.'

'Or she simply isn't mentioned,' said Stella. 'That often happens. No one mentions the hard-working wife.'

'There's one way to find out,' Iris said. 'I've got the email address. You could send Yves an email. Oh no! Are you having a heart attack now?'

'No. But if this carries on, I might. Why would I send him an email after fifty-five years? And what would I even say if I did?'

'You could start with "Hello, Yves. This is Stella Pinkheart. Do you remember me?" And see where it goes from there.'

Chapter 26

Not only was Stella persuaded to seriously consider sending an email to Yves, having finally opened up and told her secret, she also mentioned him to Marian during their next video call. Marian was both shocked and thrilled when Stella regaled her with the story.

'And the farm's in Menton?' Marian said. 'We're going there in a couple of days. One of our charter guests wants to see the lemons. Apparently Menton lemons are famous now, as is the olive oil. A lot of restaurants all over the world order them. Shall I see if we can visit Yves' place? I could take a look around and ask about the wife. Oh Stella, this will be fun. I'll tell Parker and we'll get something sorted out. It is okay if I tell Parker isn't it?'

'Yes of course. Now the secret's out of the bag I don't think it matters who knows. For years I thought it did. But it really doesn't.'

'And I've got a great idea,' Marian said. 'Why don't you come out here at the end of the season? We'll take a short trip on the yacht and we can call into Menton and see Yves.'

'Oh goodness! I'm not sure I could do that. For one, I can't remember the last time I got on a plane. For another, I'm not sure my pension would stretch to that. And for another, the last thing you and Parker want is to have to put up with an old woman trying to stand upright on a yacht. It's a lovely idea, Marian, but I don't think it would be feasible.'

'Of course it would. Getting on a plane is easy. Forget about your pension. You've done so much for me over the years and now that I'm in business with Archer I've got some cash to spare. I'll happily pay for everything. Even getting a passport, because I don't suppose you've got one if you haven't travelled for a long time. As for standing upright on a yacht. Don't even try. Just go with the flow.'

'I couldn't ask you to pay for me. You and Archer bought me this laptop. And that was so generous. But I do have a passport, as it happens. I loved travelling and my passport is something I've always automatically renewed.'

'Then it's settled. And so is the money. You can have it as your birthday and Christmas presents if you like. Don't argue. I want to do this. And it'll be lovely to see you again, especially here in the sunshine. We'll set something up for September. Even if nothing comes from you getting back in touch with Yves, you'll still have a wonderful time. We'll make sure of that.'

Chapter 27

'Where's the fire, Stella?' Iris said, as Stella hurried to the usual table that she, Rosie and Iris occupied whenever possible.

Stella flopped onto a chair and took several deep breaths before smiling broadly at Iris, and at Rosie who had only just arrived a few seconds or so before.

Bentley had joked that he might as well put a reserved sign on the table because the only people he ever saw sitting there, were the three of them.

'You're like those witches from that Shakespeare play,' he told Iris on Saturday morning when she arrived first.

'And you're like the ghost at the dinner in the very same play. Or you will be once I kill you for calling me a witch. And that reminds me. How are things going with Trisha?'

His grin faded a little and he shrugged. 'I don't know. I don't think I'll ever understand women. It's going well, sort of. But we haven't slept together and she says we should take things slowly. We haven't had sex for fifteen years. How much slower can we get?'

'That is a bit odd. If I met the love of my life again after fifteen years I'd be wanting to speed things up, not slow things down.'

'Yeah. I'm wondering if she thinks there could still be something going on between you and me. She's always talking about you and Scott and asking how things are going? She even asked me what you were like in bed? I started to wonder if it's you she fancies now and not me.'

'Really? I don't think I'm her type. And I still think she dislikes me. She's obviously really jealous of what happened between us though, isn't she if she keeps going on about me and Scott and sex and stuff?'

'Nina says I should be careful and not to be too upset if things don't work out. She says Trisha should realise she's lucky to have me. But I don't think Trisha feels lucky. I'm beginning to think she's not as keen on me as I hoped she was.'

'Nina's lovely. You should listen to her, Bentley. And maybe take her out for a coffee or something. Show Trisha you have options.'

'Options? Do I?'

'Yes. I think you do.'

'Okay. Well, I might do that. Oh dear. Here comes one of the other witches. Time for me to go.'

Rosie arrived, and Stella just after that.

'I have exciting news,' Stella said, once she'd controlled her breathing. 'I told Marian about Yves and she said she would be visiting Menton in a couple of days because one of their guests wanted to see the lemons. Anyway, Marian said she'd make enquiries and she did. And she spoke to Yves' son! Can you believe that? And she's arranged a tour for Monday. But that's not the best bit. The best bit is that she casually mentioned that she knew someone who had spent a year on a farm in the area. To cut a long story short, she actually got to speak to Yves. My Yves! And he remembers me. Oh goodness! I think I may be having a heart attack. Is that water? May I have some, please?'

Iris handed her the glass of water and held her free hand.

'This is fantastic, Stella, but you need to calm down.'

'Yes,' said Rosie. 'You've been in love with this man for fifty-five years. Don't drop dead now.'

Stella pulled a face. 'Thanks for your concern. I'll try not to. Okay. I think I'm fine now. It was just a panic attack, I'm sure. I'm so excited and nervous at the same time. To think that I may get to see Yves again after all these years. I can't believe it.'

'See him again?' Rosie queried. 'Oh. You mean you're going to video call him?'

'Well yes, I hope so. But no. I mean see him again. In the flesh. Oh didn't I mention that bit? Marian has invited me to stay on the yacht for a few days in September. At the end of the charter season. She said we can go to Menton. And that was before she actually spoke to Yves' son. And to Yves. I still can't quite take this all in. So much is happening so fast.'

'Wait.' Iris patted Stella's hand. 'Marian invited you to the Med and you're going to stay on the yacht in September?'

'Yes. Isn't that wonderful?'

'It's fantastic. But since then, Marian has managed to speak, not only to Yves' son, but also to the man himself? To Yves? Your Yves?'

'Yes. What is wrong with you today, Iris? You're usually so quick to pick up on things like this.'

'My head is spinning because there's so much going on. So what happens now? Yves remembers you but you haven't spoken to him yet?'

'Yes and no. He remembers me but we haven't spoken.'

'So how did Marian leave it with him?'

'Leave it with him? What do you mean?'

'I mean, after he said he remembered you, what did Marian say? Did she give him your number? Did she tell him you might call him? Did she say you'd be visiting in September and would he like to meet up?'

'Oh I see. I think she simply left it at that. She told him my name and he said he remembered me. She did tell me that I could now get in touch with him and explain that she'd told me about their conversation.'

Iris let out a sigh. 'I think I need someone to explain it to me. Okay. So do we know anything about the wife?'

'Yes! When Marian mentioned my name, she told Yves that I was still single. And he said he was surprised. And he asked her to pass on his regards when she next spoke to me, and to say that his wife had passed away two years ago. I thought I'd told you that.'

'Stella!' Iris and Rosie both yelled in unison.

'So basically,' Iris said. 'Yves has sent you a message via Marian to tell you he remembers you and that his wife is now dead. He's said hello and you haven't replied yet?'

'Oh I see what you mean. Should I call him now, do you think?'

'Absolutely! Right now. No wait. First I think we all need coffee and several calming breaths. And then we'll call him. Marian did give you the number, didn't she?'

'Yes.'

'And while we're having coffee,' Rosie said, as equally excited as Stella had been. 'I can tell you about my dinner last night with Joe and Penny.'

'Dear God,' Iris said. 'I knew we should've met in the pub. I'll need a stiff drink after all this.'

Chapter 28

Scott couldn't stop laughing on Saturday evening when Iris told him about her day.

'What happened when Stella eventually called Yves? I'm dying to know.'

'It was actually very romantic and emotional. Except we should've thought it through because video calling him from the café wasn't really the best idea. But we were all so excited.'

'You called him from the café?'

Iris nodded. 'He did laugh about it though so we know he's got a good sense of humour and I explained that we were getting Stella set up with an internet connection but it wasn't in place as yet. Anyway, she got straight through to him and they spent at least half an hour chatting. But it was amazing when they saw each other again for the first time after fifty-five years. He didn't speak for a few seconds and we all thought there was an issue with the connection so we were chatting amongst ourselves and trying to figure it out and then he said, "I can see you quite clearly Stella. There is not a problem with the connection." Why are you pulling a face?'

'Was that supposed to be a French accent?'

'Yes.'

'Really? It sounded more like Russian or something. I thought you were a voice coach?'

'I am. Shut up and listen. And now I'm not going to do the accent.'

'That's a relief.' Scott grinned as she hit him with a cushion.

'Then he said, "The problem is with me. I was mesmerised. Seeing you again after all these years and yet you are still that beautiful young woman I fell in love with." Isn't that romantic?'

'It is. What else did he say?'

'I don't know, exactly. Rosie and I left them to it, but Stella did say that he said all the right things and a lot more besides and that she will tell us one day. I don't know why she's being so coy, except that, maybe she wants to savour it and keep it to herself for a while. They're going to talk again tomorrow.'

'And Rosie and Joe?'

'That went well. Rosie says she thinks she could easily fall for him. Stella says Rosie already has but won't admit it yet. But I don't want to talk about them. I want to talk about us.'

'Me too.'

'How's the book going?'

'It's going well. Actually, let's not talk. Let's do other stuff.'

'That is music to my ears. I have heard enough talking today to last me a lifetime. I wish you could stay the night.'

'Me too. But I promised Trisha I wouldn't. She doesn't want Ava to wake up and find I'm not there. I don't want that either. But I don't have to go for a few hours. And I thought you said you'd heard enough talking.'

'I have. So shut up and kiss me.'

Chapter 29

'You're finally back,' Trisha said, glaring at Scott as he walked into the sitting room of The Lighthouse.

'What's wrong? Has something happened? Is Ava okay?' Panic set in immediately. Why would Trisha be up at 4.00 a.m?

'Ava's fine. Not that you seem to care about her lately. You're off with that bloody Iris woman every chance you get.'

'What? That's not true. What's wrong Trisha? You seem upset.'

'I am upset, Scott. Beyond upset. What do you see in her? I genuinely don't understand. She's pretty, but she's nothing special. She lives in a property owned by her parents. She only works when it suits her. She openly admits to having slept with Bentley purely for sex. And she even agrees she doesn't know the first thing about bringing up a child. She's nothing like Veronica. Why do you seem so intent on throwing everything away for a woman like that? I could go on, but frankly it's depressing me.'

'Not as much as your words are depressing me, Trisha.'

'Does that mean you're finally seeing sense?'

'Yes. But not in the way you're hoping. You've made it perfectly clear that you don't like Iris. Even before you met her you had nothing good to say about her. Iris, on the other hand, didn't say anything bad about you. She didn't try to sway the way I felt about you. Or make me see things that I might have overlooked. She genuinely hoped you and she could be friends. Maybe not close friends, but friends. She even asked me to reassure you that if the relationship between me and her developed into something serious, she would still want you in our lives. She would still consider you a part of this family. Because she knew that is how I thought of you. As part of my family, Trisha. And yet all you seem to want to do is make me see her faults. No one is perfect. Not even you. Iris openly admits that too. And I like the fact that she's open and honest and isn't governed by what people might think of her.'

'She doesn't care what people think, that's true. She believes she can do what she wants when she wants and that everyone will fall into place with her plans.'

'No. She doesn't think that at all. And if you knew her you would realise that. She doesn't try to be someone she's not. With Iris what you see is what you get. Except she does keep something hidden. The fact that she is much, much nicer than some people give her credit for. She helped an elderly friend simply because she could, not because she wanted anything in return. Not even thanks. She often helps her friends and people she cares about. And even total strangers. I've seen it with my own eyes.'

'She's got you believing she's some sort of saint.'

'No. She made it quite clear from the start that she is not a saint. You're trying to get me to believe she's some sort of devil or something. She's not. I can't understand why you dislike her so much. You've seen how good she is with Ava. You've seen how happy she makes me.'

'With sex! She uses sex to get what she wants.'

Scott shook his head. 'She doesn't. But we're going round in circles. Why can't you simply be happy for us? I'm happy for you and Bentley.'

'Bentley! Oh my God, Scott! What is the matter with you? There is no me and Bentley! Yes. I was crazy about the man, back in the day. But that was a lifetime ago. So much has happened since then. I told Veronica about him years ago and she thought I was holding a candle for him. I wasn't, but I let her think that, because it suited me to do so. But it's you, Scott. You! I used Bentley to try to make you jealous. To get you to see me as an attractive, sexy woman, instead of simply a friend. To make you realise you could lose me to another man. To make you want me for yourself. Why didn't you do that? Why didn't you want me, Scott? Me! Why weren't you jealous of Bentley?'

'Wh-what are you saying? I don't understand. Are you saying you're not in love with Bentley?'

'Of course I'm not in love with him. I'm in love with you! I was attracted to you the minute we met. I still wonder what might have happened if you'd seen me first. If I had been on time and Veronica had been late instead of the other way around. You and I would've got talking. We would've had those precious thirty minutes together to get to know one another. But you started dating her and I loved her because she was my best friend, so I couldn't do anything about it. And then she died and we were heartbroken together. You and I. And Ava. I know you loved me, Scott. I know you still do. I thought you just needed time. I thought you'd come to see that we belonged together. The three of us. A family. It's what Veronica would've wanted. It's what I want. It's what Ava wants. How can you throw all this away for some … tart?'

'That's enough! I'm not sure what's happening here, or if I've misunderstood all this in some way but I have never loved you in the way you're suggesting, Trisha. I loved you as a dear friend. I still love you as that. Although I'm beginning to think you're not such a dear friend as I thought. But I'm not attracted to you in a sexual way. I've never considered spending my life with you. I've never wanted that. And neither would Veronica. I don't think you knew her as well as you thought you did. And this is going to hurt you but after everything you've said I need to say it. Veronica would've loved Iris. And if she could speak from wherever she is right now, she would tell me to run, not walk into Iris' arms. And she'd also tell me that Iris will make a good mother to Ava. Not perfect. Even Veronica would admit she wasn't perfect. No one is. But Iris loves those she cares about with her whole heart. And she will do the best she can. And that is good enough for me. And it's good enough for Ava.

Because I'm doing the best I can too. I'm sorry if you don't like this and I'm sorry if this means you don't want to be in our lives. Perhaps, considering what you've said, that is for the best.'

'What? You can't be serious, Scott! It will break Ava's heart. It'll break my heart! Don't you care about Ava? Don't you care about me?'

'I care about Ava with every fibre of my being. She will miss you, as will I, but neither of us will be heartbroken. I'm truly sorry if you will be, but I can't pretend to feel something I don't. And have you given a moment's thought to Bentley? He's in love with you, Trisha. You're going to break his heart. Don't you care about that?'

'No! I don't.'

Scott took a deep breath and clenched his fists.

'Then this conversation is over and I think you should pack your bags and leave as soon as possible. If you think for one second that this is what Veronica would've wanted, you're completely and utterly wrong. I'll tell Ava you had to leave to start a new job and that we won't be seeing you for a while. If you can ever feel able to accept that all there could be between us is friendship, you've got my number. But please do not ever – and I do mean never – speak to me again about being in love with me. I'm going to sit with Ava until she wakes up. Don't even think about coming into her room. Because if you do I will physically remove you.'

'Scott! No! Don't go! Please! Let's talk about this. I need you to see Iris is wrong for you. Completely wrong for you.'

'And I need you to see she's right for me. In fact, she's perfect for me. Goodbye Trisha. I truly wish you all the best. I hope you'll have the decency to speak to Bentley before you leave.'

She reached out and grabbed his arm but he shook off her hand, marched from the room and closed the door behind him.

Chapter 30

'Bentley can't believe it,' Iris said flopping onto the chair and gratefully taking the large glass of wine that Scott handed her. 'No one can. El and Archer actually considered coming back when they heard, but Bentley wouldn't hear of it. He said he'll be fine, once he's got over the shock, but none of us believed him. Until Nina appeared and wrapped her arms around him, and then we all saw the light.'

'Saw the light?' Scott knelt down in front of her and looked her in the eyes.

Iris took a gulp of wine, let out a relieved sigh and nodded. 'Yes. Bentley is better off without Trisha and deep down, he knows that. He and Nina have been getting on like a house on fire and I don't think it'll be long until he asks her out on a date.'

'Harley's aunt? I like her. She seems extremely caring and level-headed. And she's pretty.' He grinned. 'Not as pretty as you, obviously.'

'Obviously.' Iris laughed. 'I think they clicked from day one when she came to help. If Trisha hadn't popped up on that Friday night, I truly believe that he and Nina would be dating by now.'

'The problem is, he's been hurt. It might make him a little more cautious and unwilling to jump back in with someone else. Even someone as lovely as Nina.'

'It might. But I'll be having words with him and so will Stella and Rosie, so he'll soon start to realise he had a lucky escape and that he mustn't let Nina slip away.'

'And you can be very persuasive. I can speak from experience.'

'Did you need persuading?'

He laughed and shook his head. 'No. You had me the moment you screamed and told me to "Back off" and I saw your face in the moonlight. Although you did lie to me.'

'I thought you were a mugger. The lies were justified.'

He leant forward and kissed her on the forehead.

'I should still be working on the book but I'd much rather be doing something else.'

'Cooking dinner?'

'Nope.' He kissed her on the nose.

'Collecting Ava from Stella's?'

'Nah-huh. You know we said we'd collect her at 6 p.m. on the dot and it's only a little after 2 right now.' He kissed her left cheek.

'Helping me with the laundry?'

'Absolutely not.' He kissed her on the other cheek.

'Then I'm running out of things for you to do.'

'Oh you are, are you?' He kissed her on the mouth.

'And places on my face for you to kiss me.'

'I can think of lots of things I could do. And lots more places I could kiss you.' He kissed her on her neck.

'I like the sound of that and I definitely like the direction in which these kisses are heading. But what about your book?'

'What book?' He kissed her collarbone.

'The thriller you're supposed to be working on.'

'I can think of something far more thrilling to work on.' He kissed her décolletage.

'But you said you wanted to finish a chapter today and finish the whole book before you leave Clementine Cove.'

'That's still over two weeks away. And besides, I've been thinking about that.' He lifted up her jumper and kissed her stomach.

'So have I.'

He raised his head and met her eyes.

'I don't want to leave. I know we've got two more weeks but I mean after that. I don't want to leave Clementine Cove. I don't want to leave you. I know we'll still see one another and I know it will work. But I love it here. And Ava loves it too. She's really happy here. Especially with Stella. She and Stella have really hit it off. I think Ava prefers Stella to Trisha, which is weird but fantastic.'

'Then don't leave. I'm happy you and Ava are here. I'll be unhappy if you leave. I know we said London isn't far and we'd see one another often, but it feels like a million miles away whenever I think about you going back. And I've already told you that you can stay here for as long as you and Ava want to. You can move out of The Lighthouse and into here right now. Today. If you want to. If you want to stay.'

'I want to stay.'

'Then stay. I want you to. But you're getting behind on your kisses. From my count, that's two you owe me already.'

'And this makes three. And I'm a man who always pays up.'

He slid his fingers inside her waistband and popped the top button of her jeans.

'I love a man who pays his debts.'

'And I love you, Iris Talbot.'

'Wait!' She put her hand on his. 'You love me?'

He furrowed his brows. 'Yes. Is that a problem?'

'You're kidding right?'

He tensed visibly. 'About loving you? No.'

Iris laughed. 'No. I meant you're kidding about it being a problem, aren't you? Because I love you too, Scott Fitzgerald. I love you with all of my heart. And Ava too. And believe me, that's something I never expected to happen.'

'I never expected any of this to happen. I only came here because I had writer's block and because Ava's school had asbestos. I thought it would be a few weeks of me bashing out a novel and spending time on the beach with Ava. I never expected to meet the woman I'd want to spend the rest of my life with. But I have.'

'And that's me?'

'Of course, it's you. Although Stella comes a very close second.'

Iris laughed and threw her arms around his neck.

'Oh Scott. I'm so glad I walked home along the beach that Friday night. I love you so, so much.'

'And I love you just as much. Now let me catch up with my kisses will you? Where was I?'

'Undoing the top button of my jeans.'

'Ah yes. So I was.'

'But will you say you love me just one more time. Because it sounds so good.'

'I'll say it as often as you like. And I'll still be saying it when we're Stella's age and beyond. I love you, Iris Talbot.'

Coming soon

Please see my website for details.
www.emilyharvale.com

You can sign up for my newsletter while you're there, and also play book related games and puzzles in the Games Room of my Open House.

A Note from Emily

A little piece of my heart goes into every one of my books and when I send them on their way, I really hope they bring a smile to someone's face. If this book made you smile, or gave you a few pleasant hours of relaxation, I'd love you to tell your friends.

And if you have a minute or two to post a review (just a few words will do) or even simply a rating, that would be lovely too. Reviews help other readers choose an author's books, which is why we're always asking you lovely readers to do them. Huge thanks to those of you who do so, and for your wonderful comments and support on social media. Thank you.

A writer's life can be lonely at times. Sharing a virtual cup of coffee or a glass of wine, or exchanging a few friendly words via my website Open House, or on Facebook, Twitter or Instagram is so much fun.

You can sign up for my newsletter too. It's absolutely free, your email address is safe and won't be shared and I won't bombard you, I promise. You can enter competitions and enjoy some giveaways. In addition to that, there's my author page on Facebook.

There's also my lovely, Facebook group and now my wonderful, Emily's Open House (both mentioned earlier) where you'll find free book-related games and puzzles, meet me, and other fans, and get access to my book news, sometimes early extracts from my books and lots more besides. You'll find all my contact links on my website and in the Contact section in this book. Hope to chat with you soon.

I can't wait to bring you more stories that I hope will capture your heart, mind and imagination, allowing you to escape into a world of romance in some enticingly beautiful settings.

To see all my books, please go to the books page on my website.

Also by Emily Harvale

The Golf Widows' Club
Sailing Solo
Carole Singer's Christmas
Christmas Wishes
A Slippery Slope
The Perfect Christmas Plan
Be Mine
It Takes Two
Bells and Bows on Mistletoe Row

Lizzie Marshall series:
Highland Fling – book 1
Lizzie Marshall's Wedding – book 2

Goldebury Bay series:
Ninety Days of Summer – book 1
Ninety Steps to Summerhill – book 2
Ninety Days to Christmas – book 3

Hideaway Down series:
A Christmas Hideaway – book 1
Catch A Falling Star – book 2
Walking on Sunshine – book 3
Dancing in the Rain – book 4

Hall's Cross series
Deck the Halls – book 1
The Starlight Ball – book 2

Michaelmas Bay series
Christmas Secrets in Snowflake Cove – book 1
Blame it on the Moonlight – book 2

Lily Pond Lane series
The Cottage on Lily Pond Lane – four-part serial
Part One – New beginnings
Part Two – Summer secrets
Part Three – Autumn leaves
Part Four – Trick or treat
Christmas on Lily Pond Lane
Return to Lily Pond Lane
A Wedding on Lily Pond Lane
Secret Wishes and Summer Kisses on Lily Pond Lane

Wyntersleap series
Christmas at Wynter House – Book 1
New Beginnings at Wynter House – Book 2
A Wedding at Wynter House – Book 3
Love is in the Air – spin off

Merriment Bay series
Coming Home to Merriment Bay – Book 1
(four-part serial)
Part One – A Reunion
Part Two – Sparks Fly
Part Three – Christmas
Part Four – Starry Skies
Chasing Moonbeams in Merriment Bay – Book 2
Wedding Bells in Merriment Bay – Book 3

Seahorse Harbour series
Summer at my Sister's – book 1
Christmas at Aunt Elsie's – book 2
Just for Christmas – book 3
Tasty Treats at Seahorse Bites Café – book 4
Dreams and Schemes at The Seahorse Inn – book 5
Weddings and Reunions in Seahorse Harbour – book 6

Clementine Cove series
Christmas at Clementine Cove – book 1
Broken Hearts and Fresh Starts at Cove Café – book 2

To see a complete list of my books, or to sign up for my newsletter, go to
www.emilyharvale.com/books

If you really love my books and want to be the first to see some sneak peeks, play book related games and connect with Emily and other fans, you can ask to become a Harvale Heart and gain a virtual key to Emily's Open House.
www.emilyharvale.com/MembersClub

There's also an exclusive Facebook group for fans of my books.
www.emilyharvale.com/FacebookGroup

Or scan the QR code below to see all my books on Amazon.

Stay in touch with

Emily Harvale

If you want to be the first to hear Emily's news, find out about book releases, see covers and maybe chat with other fans, there are a few options for you:

Visit: www.emilyharvale.com

and subscribe to Emily's newsletter via the 'sign me up' box. Or, if you really love Emily's books, apply to join Emily's Open House here:

www.emilyharvale.com/MembersClub

Or ask to join Emily's exclusive Facebook Group here:

www.emilyharvale.com/FacebookGroup

Alternatively, just come and say 'Hello' on social media:

- @EmilyHarvaleWriter
- @EmilyHarvale
- @EmilyHarvale

Printed in Great Britain
by Amazon